Esp 'is a well-woven, dimensional tale: well and (and a lively, colloquial ver crisp, fluid, elegant; robust and energeuc. ... narrative voice and persona, too, are as appealingly accessible as they are well-articulated, effectively and vibrantly alive; compellingly, persuasively drawn out. I was especially struck—and impressed—by three elements: the very knowledgeable familiarity, richness and fluency of the story's command of Grenadian slang and vernacular nuance; the various and distinct (and distinctively blended) musical and pop cultural traditions and inflections they invoke; and, overall, the vivid (dramatic, metaphorical, and tonal), original and effective narrative mobilization in the tale. No small feat, and a very solid, enviable achievement.'

Roberto Márquez, William J. Kenan Jr. Professor of Latin American and Caribbean Studies, Mount Holyoke College, Massachusetts, author of *A World Among These Islands: Essays on Literature, Race and National Identity in Antillean America.*

'There's some damn fine channelling at work there, a really impressive feat of cultural translation. I also don't think that it's cultural or postcolonial appropriation: this novella speaks truths about growing up, and understanding the bonds of friendship and community, that are applicable to any social and cultural group. It could just as well have been set in Poland or the Philippines. The common factor is that the setting of *Esp* contains the shadowy recent history of a stronger power taking a hand in local politics. This offsets the uneasy sense of being a client nation, a country that is still too close to colonisation to be properly independent.'

Kate Macdonald on *Esp*, UK Novella Award, 2015.

'*The Portswick Imp* for me was both a pleasure and a challenge to read...Thomas's writing is engaging and beautiful but it is also clever... I felt the emotions of the characters and I was reading the last pages through tears.'

Sally Shaw, review of *The Portswick Imp* for *Sabotage Reviews*, 2020.

Sing Ho! Stout Cortez

Novellas and Stories

Michael W. Thomas

Sing Ho! Stout Cortez
Novellas and Stories
by
Michael W. Thomas

First published in 2021 by Black Pear Press
www.blackpear.net

ISBN 978-1-913418-54-0
Cover design Ted Eames

Black Pear Press

Dedication:

Again to Lynda, with heartfelt gratitude. To Tony Girling and Barry George, for unwavering friendship.

About Sing Ho! Stout Cortez:

All of these pieces were written between 2014 and 2020. The earliest, *Esp*, was shortlisted for the UK Novella Award, 2015, and enlarges on the experiences of Henderson Bray, first encountered in 'Misshapes from Cadbury's' in my story collection, *The Portswick Imp*. An early working title for the present collection was *Timely Voices*. What seemed to unite the pieces here was the sense that, in each, the narrator or main character works towards (or stumbles upon) a crucial time in their life: a time to discover, confront, act or somehow honour a long-standing rendezvous with something—a feeling, a nugget of knowledge—whose importance can no longer be dodged. I think that such a theme still holds good. Reading through the pieces again, however, I'm also struck by another one: escape from current circumstance. In some pieces, characters literally do just that (all hail to the car and the open road). Of course, once a story ends, it's lights out and curtain. But it's been observed that every exit becomes an entrance elsewhere. So I can only hope that, however these characters act, whatever prompts their changes or departures, they will find what they're looking for (or something as near as makes, in the end, no difference).

Michael W. Thomas, Summer 2021.

Contents

Esp: The Voice of Grenada
Henderson Bray's Account
A novella

Maurice Bishop, Prime Minister of Grenada from 1979 to 1983, had a Marxist cast of mind. He established Workers' Councils throughout the nation. Communism made itself more tangibly felt through aid from the Soviet Union and Cuba, which resulted in the construction of a runway to facilitate Grenada's tourism. But Bishop had a politician's sense of balance, a fear of any rocky boats, so strove to maintain good relations with the US. Bernard Coard, his Finance Minister, shared neither this vision of détente nor Bishop's commitment to grassroots democracy. On 19th October, 1983, he overthrew Bishop in a military coup. US response was swift, an initial wave of troops landing in Grenada on 25th October. Over several days, the Grenadian army battled fiercely but, swelling rapidly from 1,200 to 7,000, the invaders overcame them. Surrender or flight to the mountains were the only options for the home force.

The UN General Assembly subsequently condemned the invasion as an unlawful intervention in the affairs of a sovereign state. Discussed in the Security Council, the consequent resolution looked set for enshrinement till the US vetoed it.

Now this story is not invented, and reality is always more complex than invention: less kempt, cruder, less rounded out. It rarely relies on one level.

—Primo Levi, *The Periodic Table*

1

Preface

I love the voices. But sometimes I wish there were two of me. One still propped in a chair outside the Bray house, or on a hotel balcony with a reasonable view of the road into Harford Village. Catching all the voices, smoothing them, dressing them in their best—only then sending them to the other one, this me, the roamer. That way, I might be able to roam without the ambush of midge-storms at my neck, in my head, each needle of sound another person, a different emotion, a reminder of how lives still turn this way and that far away from me, how I can only bear a deflected witness.

But no…I love the voices. I love how they arrange themselves. A letter from home is my mother's voice, but standing behind her is a line of others, each waiting its cue: she quotes one directly, paraphrases another, gilds rumination with scraps of a third. Some are dignified, others antsy, but all defer to my mother: the whipper-in, the chucker-out. A letter from a friend is full of his odd angles, the tics of the pen that call him their own. Again, though, other voices wait, perhaps a bit pushy, sometimes demanding he let them in before his own news, instead of it. No deference then. My friend doesn't whip or chuck. He holds the coats…

I love the voices. It's just that, sometimes, they come as if their only gifts to me are bafflement, loneliness.

1

7, Coneygreane Place, Hagley, Worcestershire, England.

I'd become so used to getting mail for the previous occupants that, when the letterbox made its usual row, I assumed that someone else—a furniture store, a credit outfit, some wing of this country's formidable leisure industry—was seeking their patronage, or perhaps reminding them that the cost of previous patronage was overdue.

Out I went to the hall, playing my usual game. Would the shiny little address boxes be calling for David and June Bedworth, or for David alone? For a while now, it had just been David, but I lived in hope. Perhaps both names would shine forth again, declaring that they'd made up but, in their excess of rediscovered joy, had still neglected to redirect their mail. This is how it can be when you're in a new country. Friends and family in abeyance, you busy yourself with surmise about strangers, especially if they don't seem so strange, if accident invites you to claim an intimacy with them. The Bedworths were long gone, but still their names had fallen easy on the rope-work mat that Thelma next door had given me. It was as though I'd been instructed to keep an eye on other lives: to pay them an attention which, though uninformed, was no less worthy of care. Now and then I re-posted what came, with *No longer at this address*, as kindly but emphatically advised by Harold next door. This changed nothing. I could, I suppose, have enquired about the Bedworths from him and Thelma. The name had come up fleetingly in our talks, and I'd interpreted their 'Tchahs' and rolled eyes as an invitation to probe further. But I preferred to meet the Bedworths on my own fantastical terms. I didn't want to know that they'd had raucous parties, or that she was flighty, or he abusive. I even considered a day when the letterbox clanged and I saw a man's bulk spread vaguely against the frosted glass: David Bedworth himself, warm of handshake, teary of eye, apologising for any inconvenience caused by my role as interim postie, bending his head a little as he whispered, 'She's come round—we're back together, pal.' Pal: I always tagged that on.

Today, though, there was one letter alone, for me. Franked by sundry nations, it had travelled further than I had. The stamps were more smudge than artwork. They might have been the profile of a great name from my country's past—if such had been agreed on—but black lines wove thickly about what could have been a head. All over the envelope, questions were eloquent on the letter's struggle to reach me. *Zone A, KN, Jam? NY? Not for Mount Pleasant. Try Wolves? Try Wolves Worcs?* But despite officialdom's graffiti and even after all this time, I recognised the blocky writing, the bestowal of an extra 's' on my first name.

I went back into the living room and sat down. Outside, the morning was at its Saturday speed. But all I could hear was the Voice of Grenada, and all I could see was the boy who owned it.

2

Esp—Paul Belmar, but his real name had retreated to his birth certificate and moments of maternal wrath, thanks to Restless Headey, devil of the Caribbean, at that time taking passable human shape as our English teacher. Headey despaired of us boys as a matter of routine. He certainly despaired of me, a situation compounded by his undefined friendship with my father. (The only plus there was that, far from beaching me in exile, it actually secured my peers' sympathy.)

But he reserved his prize bewilderment for Paul. Gallons of ink, too: Paul's compositions would return looking like the rout of serenity, his blue falling back under Headey's red. *Rein in your punctuation, esp. dashes. Where are your tenses off to, boy? Keep that woefully overdue date with my verb-worksheets, esp. pluperfect. This is meant to be a third-person narrative, Belmar. You've conscripted an army to describe Jekyll's laboratory—I, you, he (no she, Belmar? Is science still the land of the macho?). Refresh your memory about (or mayhap introduce it to) the essentials of narration, esp. consistent voice. 'Las, 'las, Belmar* (a theft, this word, from his beloved John Webster)—*this out-contempts contempt.*

Such dressings-down didn't faze Paul. A happy pluralism drove his creativity. Why shouldn't a single sentence stop off at all tenses? Why shouldn't a whole mess of viewpoints get all edgy about Jekyll's lab? A dash was a chance to catch breath, a groove between tracks on vinyl. A dash told everything after to wait its turn—that it wasn't so big, or why wasn't it heading up the sentence?

Headey was a lagahou[1] sinking his undead fangs in pure, free words, a bellhop jumping to the tetchy commands of dowager-grammar. He knew nothing.

But Paul's *esps* made him proud. He tracked them like a pitcher might track his strike-rate, and his pride infected the rest of us. It became clear that he was setting esp-targets for the week, month, term. Eric Mitchell, a lugubrious economist, started running a book, allowing a margin of two either side of Paul's likely total in a given period. Once I won five dollars, splitting it with Paul, the engine of this random largesse. Whether he looked at Headey's worksheets, even to check how deliciously far he'd ranged from them, we never knew. But his real name decayed on the school air, only kept twitchily alive by those who faced us at the front of a class or the occasional summons from Principal Tutela. In our world—child of and exile from the school around it—Esp he became and remained.

But the Voice of Grenada? There was no warning that he'd take that name on alongside Esp. Or perhaps there was. There was joyous noise, certainly. There was contraband. And again, there was Headey.

When he wasn't desolating English, Esp was into the guitar. He got pretty good, too. Like his tenses, his favourite players came from all over. But there was no face among them from any Caribbean island, no Dwight Pinkney, no Fitzroy Coleman or Flores Chaviano. His heroes came from lands where, we thought, folk had permanent colds or got moved on by the cops for

---

[1] Blood-sucker, vampire.

looking like that instead of this; then, too, they were coeval with our older brothers, our youngest dads, which made them even mistier. Eric Clapton and Jimi Hendrix tussled for Esp's golden crown, though they got shunted off by times in favour of, say, Pete Townshend's windmill arm or the precise snap of Mark Knopfler. And he went yet further, in time and oddity. My Uncle Padmore, a limited but flamboyant picker himself, got wind of Esp's doings and dug out a cassette of Les Paul and Mary Ford whose quality spoke of a mike prodded against a mono-speaker:

'Pass him this. "How High The Moon," boy. One listen and he'll be flying there.'

He was right. Their take on the song enraptured Esp—the whole swamp-toned album did. He saw a giddying challenge in Les Paul's multi-track wizardry. Clapton and the rest were great, no doubt of it, but they played one guitar. There were times when they defied it, outraged it, melted it, but it was still just a single thing in their hands. This Les Paul, said Esp…and his wonderment would stream out in a long whistle. He became the pioneer's gospeller.

The business of reproducing what Les Paul had wrought with miles of tape—who knows, even cried over, while Mary supplied beer and handkerchiefs—didn't faze Esp in the least. At an audition for a school show, he constructed a singular *hommage* to 'How High The Moon', playing a tape he'd recorded of the chord progression and then—with art and elegance, we esp-target gamblers thought—playing the same progression live but with a sweetly-timed delay to catch something of the original's fat echoes. Now and then he threw in mouth-guitar, a line of *juvva-da-juv-juvs* which jostled sparkily with the live chords.

Such thickset beauty was lost on Flutter Priestman, the flugelhorn-playing music teacher:

'And the words, Mr Belmar?' he called from the well of the hall. 'Something to stop the *juv-juvs* getting lonely?'

Esp said the words would be right along for the second audition and he was told he wouldn't get one.

'Headey got to that bol'face,' he declared after.[2] Somewhere in his eyes, it seemed, was the inkling of another challenge.

Priestman's rebuff spurred him to put a band together. Eric Mitchell, lugubrious esp-target bookie, had some musical clue and prowled around on acoustic bass. A kid called Twinko, already famed (and frequently carpeted) for clattering any available surface, was lured away from lunch tables and vulnerable heads and parked behind a half-complete kit.

'And the name?' we asked, after they'd tried out a few times.

'Been keeping it cool and dark,' hissed Esp, 'all set for the reveal'—which was now.

'Ah-sah,'[3] groaned Twinko, chucking two invisible sticks at the ceiling. Eric's shoulders trembled.

We tried convincing Esp that 'The Rock Exponents' was truly awful, a name that a Headey or Priestman would dream up. Perhaps thinking of the esp-targets he

---

[2] Bol'face: a pushy person.

[3] Cry of despair, exasperation.

handled like market stocks, Eric suggested 'Future Tense', explaining its power to Esp one lunchtime. As usual, he sounded diffident yet assured, proving once again that, of all of us, he would stroll calmly up to a great future and, all courtesy, shake its hand. 'Future Tense', said Eric, spoke of the edgy, unknown days to come as so many powder-kegs: the '83 invasion but without American shouts or mountains of empty Bud-bottles. Twinko clapped Eric's shoulder, insisting that he was right, his suggestion was properly out there.

Esp wasn't having it. More, he announced that the band was on a swerve away from Les, Jimi, the lot. Masters all, they were, no doubt of it, but a true Rock Exponent was no one's servant: 'We ain't doing tribute-band arseness. Chou poule!'[4] Eric and Twinko exchanged 'now what comes?' glances.

What came was Esp, songwriter. 'If You Don't Love Me' was the first. Now, in this distant living-room, safe from the rain whose thin come-again, go-again I still found hard to accept, I let the whole thing shake through my head like a night-train.

Unsurprisingly, Esp's disavowal of tribute-rock came with some slack. Half of 'If You Don't Love Me' was a straight lift from Roy Orbison's 'In Dreams'. This, once again, was Uncle Padmore. After the Les Paul triumph, he saw himself as a deep-field Svengali:

'Try that sparky boy with these'—and now he pressed Orbison's *Golden Greats* into my hand, predicting a bigger bang than with Les Paul. He was right—'In Dreams' sent

---

[4] To hell with that!

9

Esp beyond Les and Mary's moon:

'Man, I love that jump,' he'd say, as Roy crested the last verse. 'That jump I must have.' And he did, tying onto it words which, completely missing the original's sweet heartbreak, still made a virtue of his cut-and-dried view of life, of love:

If you don't love me

If you don't love me

I'll hide away in some foreign land

Where nobody can contraband.

Perhaps the idea of Esp as the Voice of Grenada was seeded there, in that last foolish-sounding line. He got in quick enough with an explanation, one which drew more *ah-sahs* from Twinko but made Eric narrow his eyes, as though Esp were a book he'd skimmed far too quickly. For starters, said Esp, this was and wasn't a love song. OK, 'contraband' could mean, as he put it, 'heart-stuff and mess—but I'm talking history, too, all 'long the C'ribbean.' Not fancy-dress pirates, he assured us, no 'Avast there' simmy-dimmy.[5] He meant Europe's long piracy, its game of slice-and-dice in our islands.

'See?' He grinned deep and warm into our astonishment. 'Two levels, like Headey scribblers go in for with all that "Let's hang at the ha-ha, lady-friend" and "there's problematics in the fall of a sparrow" and—t'ing on t'ing.'[6]

---

[5] Mumbo-jumbo.

[6] Et cetera.

We thought he was expecting a lot of 'contraband'. We hadn't had the benefit of the Sixties, whose happy dishevelment would have allowed us much wow-ing and far out-ing. But Eric moved his lips noiselessly, turning the word round and round, seeming to emphasise a different syllable each time. He looked again at Esp, hard, as though the boy had morphed from face-in-crowd to prince. If any of us had any depths to which 'contraband' spoke, it would be Eric. And there was still verse two to write.

Next morning, Eric arrived with a neatly-written effort that put the song on a whole other footing. It was rather longer than Esp's verse. Now, 'If You Don't Love Me' was addressed to conquistadors, bibulous milords, peak-capped Dutchmen, pictured among goblets and favourites, turning their attention to the slave-shoals of Africa and thence, in the last line, to 'the swart plantation miles' of the Caribbean. I loved 'swart'. I hadn't a clue what it meant and didn't want to know—it was a Mitchell word and that was enough. It belonged. And the whole thing, we reckoned, would bring the song in at easily three minutes—more.

But Esp had a verse of his own. He appeared while we were still marvelling at Eric's, pressed in with his own bit of paper and began to sing. Eric broke the silence: 'Do it again,' he said and studied the words as Esp, upping the *brio,* obliged. I studied Eric, almost hearing the tick of his thoughts, the whirr of an attitude being turned about. He looked up. Had his gaze been a movie close-up, there might have been two tiny Esps in his eyes, heads flip-flopping like Paul McCartney's. But in this real moment they dulled over. To his mind, it seemed, Esp had only been prince for a day.

It was easy to see why, especially with our heads stuffed full of conquistadors and the rest. 'On the other hand,' began Esp's verse. If he'd stopped right there—on a teaser, like his beloved dashes—we could still have guessed what followed. And it did. Say the girl loved him. Well, he'd stay put. No foreign land would bear his footprint. In the last line of his new verse 'contraband' just hung there, a big word in a bunch of filler, like *come away today* or *I want a chance to dance in France.* No long-dead milord would find it worrying at his eternal sleep.

Ah, but we were kids. What did we know? Well, about hope, for one, and I was certainly hopeful when, beaming on us, Esp finished his second go, Eric went to give back his paper and Twinko stayed his hand:

'You check this out, Esp. This is hot'—and Eric's poetry lay in Esp's palm.

Esp read it through, holding the page like a map that might need turning round. At last he stabbed down his finger:

'What's catamite?'

I had some vague notion, enough to feel a bit edgy about voicing it in the patrolled space of school. But Eric pitched in. Sounding like a dictionary with heart, he explained, his words robust but diplomatic. We didn't snigger. Esp nodded and the nod went round. I saw new possibilities: a time, perhaps, when we could take 'The Rock Exponents' away from him like an over-chewed teddy and rename the band ...well, just about anything. But then—

'Headey write this? Does he know? Bon Jay,[7] is he into us?' Esp couldn't resist a James Brown spin on the spot, eyes sparkling at the notion of the foe seduced. There were groans, *ah-sahs* all round. A bristle of fingers pointed at Eric. Abashed for a second, Esp goggled, gave him a loose salute:

'That some essay, my man. But, look, the song…it's already got its trajection.' God knows where he got that word from: it sounded like a Headey misfire.

Then came the petulance of the morning bell. As we broke up, Twinko twitched his head at Eric:

'Keep comin' up with that stuff. Marley, Toots, they'd get it.' His brother Ambrose, he added, had left his guitar behind when he went to Venezuela. 'You have it. Get some chords down. No use to me.' He flipped back his palms: 'All my noise is right here.' Far ahead of us, Esp was shucking and jiving, singing his second verse, repeating 'contraband' over and over. Foreign land, contraband. Love and dove. Moon and June.

---

[7] Good God.

3

One of the things that fascinated us about Esp was how an idea would flower in his head. So it was with the gorgeously irrational notion that Restless Headey knew of and was into the Exponents. Reason suffered early, inevitable defeats. How did we know he hadn't heard them? That lagahou was a sneaker and slider about. Some shadow back of the yard any time they rehearse, how to say that wasn't him? How? Over the next few days, we knew that something was at large behind those big eyes. It burst out when Headey spoke of free composition.

Every so often, Headey suffered us to turn in our own inventions. In madcap moments, he even let us stray from bib-and-tucker prose. This was possibly because he enjoyed the drama of handing back such efforts. Wide of eye, gurning in apparent pain, he would pace the lines of desks and put the pages straight into our hands, foregoing the usual ritual in which we'd approach the front Oliver Twist-style and have them thrust at our chests like fake money. He was noticeably lighter on his feet when he did this pacing. Perhaps he imagined that, letting us loose with our own thoughts, he'd invited a second fall of Jericho and was poised to get out before the stones crashed. We'd never yet sold his despair short.

On the day of Headey's latest invitation to be free, Esp was beside himself: 'See?' he said as we walked home. 'He's heard the Exponents. He wants full proof.'

Twinko clapped hand to forehead: 'You think he lay this on so you can go cabaret?'

'I'm breaking down the enemy.' Esp capered about us and suddenly the Harford air was filled with nobody's idea of Sean Connery: *'You want me to talk, Mr Headey? No, Mr Bond, I want you to siiing.'*

'Then you sing solo, brar.[8] He ain't have drum and noisiness in there. Me and Eric try, he fatigue[9] us good.'

Esp jiggled a high hand: solo was his intent.

'How you know he allow you?'

'No choice! Fascination!'

Eric ducked in to catch Esp's eye: 'It's the contraband song, right?'

'Bon Jay, you Mitchell—what else?'

'You need write t'ing like "Redemption Song" or "Many Rivers to Cross,"' advised Twinko, winking at Eric. 'That'd pop Headey boils.'

Esp unwound himself from his caper and turned solemn:

'Ah-sah, those guys are OK on a middling road, but I got—' His body inflated into James Brown splendour again, and 'If You Don't Love Me' set the birds complaining. As he went at it, Twinko leaned to Eric:

'I cleaned up Ambrose guitar. Call by.'

On a Friday morning, we submitted what we'd done. Headey dished them out the following Monday afternoon, all gurning face and tiptoe, giving us to understand he'd spent the weekend with demons in his soul. Mine, like most, bore the regulation comments.

Eric's didn't. He'd apparently turned the rejected verse of 'If You Don't Love Me' into a play, a two-hander, which Headey commanded him and Twinko to

---

[8] Brother.
[9] Give us hell.

act out. Maybe they'd rehearsed it. Certainly, Twinko shifted with ease from his usual barging talk.

There were two characters: a conquistador and an English milord, in their cups in a hall dripping gold, created through brisk exposition and careful dumb-show. A huge map was propped before them, Eric flinging his hands wide and deep to show its dimensions, then laying it out on Headey's table. They spoke of their countries' power and the coming ages. Variously, they played blackjack, rolled dice, tossed coins, each switch of game signalled by a subtly percussive Twinko. No rancour attended the gaming. The two nobles applauded each other's way with Lady Luck, commiserated when she turned moody. Now and then, one or other rose to mark lines on the map. Sport over, Eric and Twinko made a big to-do of turning the map round for the rest of us. The remaining dialogue gave us to understand that it was our necklace, Grenada and its neighbour pearls, now split fifty-fifty between Spain and England. Beneath her caprices, it seemed, Lady Luck had been even of hand. Some final, back-slappy exchanges derided the aspirations of inferior powers. Fun was had at the expense of clogs, berets, spineless jellyfish in the Lisbon roads. With one last dramatic gesture—rare for Eric, par for the course with Twinko—they locked arms, drank deep from their goblets and cried *To The Morrow!*

The boys resumed their seats amid wild applause, from those who got what was going on, from those who didn't but guessed that, somehow, Eric had played Headey at his own lofty game. A few of us, me included, clapped a bit but then just stared at Headey's table—still

16

draped, it seemed, with that map of division. A teasing confusion infected me. There it was, there it wasn't. For a moment, I felt that our country didn't exist, that its history had been a matter of coming and going, a Caribbean Brigadoon waiting on the roll of the dice. We'd been keeping the land warm till the next wave of purchasers turned up. Maybe we still were.

Then I found myself leaning across with the others nearest Eric to see what mark he'd got. Whistles told our amazement. We looked at Headey: a Headey transformed, as he seemed to be, shaking his head as though unable to believe what he'd just seen, to credit that he'd given a mark like that, withheld even a stroke of red ink. Had Eric's effort not been half as good, Headey's old self would have stayed comfortably in its skin, tartly observing that Anglo-Hispanic relations had been something other than presented. But this Headey was in a mist, and I remembered that he'd led the clapping when the play was done.

I felt a glow: happiness on Eric's behalf, yes, but also because he'd salvaged 'swart' from the verse Esp had dismissed, the germ of what we'd just witnessed. That Eric word again, mysterious and beautiful. As a symbol, perhaps, of his characters' bizarre fair play, he'd given the word to milord and conquistador alike.

A chair scraped. There was deep sighing. The only other boy put on notice to perform was getting itchy. He worked his shoulders, stared ahead unseeing, like a headline entertainer unsettled by some upstart act at the bottom of the bill. At last it came: the slow, robotic crook of Headey's finger. Esp jaunted to the front of the room.

'Read,' said the old Headey. Those of us in the know choked back sniggers. Read? Man, how could he get it so wrong? And him deep into the Exponent vibe besides? Esp flourished his paper—I thought he might mop his brow with it—stepped away from the man's silly command, pocketed the paper and went tight into himself. 'Oh, daddy,' sighed Twinko and, as if his murmur were a pre-arranged signal, Esp turned a Presley snarl upon the most outrageous English teacher in the Caribbean and took off.

It was image pressed on image, all the greats working as one in the boy's body. Johnny Ray ('The Nabob of Sob', as my Uncle Padmore routinely added) scrunched his limbs, forcing a drop to one knee. Elvis had him up again, flung him wide, played flame about his hips. Lord Kitchener leaned in smilingly for a moment of shoulder-rolling calypso, and then it was Mop-Top time, Esp simultaneously as puppyish as McCartney, as intense as Lennon. A cape of air wrapped about his shoulders (in his own mind, no doubt, twice the size of Eric's map), and he tore it off, then another, then another, each spun and discarded in move-perfect homage to James Brown's fake endings when he sang 'Prisoner of Love'. For the final lines, Orbison stilled him, made him older and wiser. I'd say we all thrilled to how he delivered 'contraband' for the very last time, making it vibrate Big O-style so it spoke of all the lessons taught and learned in this dirty old vexatious world. Then he stood silent before us, bulked and centred, a leader of men.

I thought about the sight I'd had of Esp's paper when Headey gave it back—all that ravening ink. The line, 'I'll

18

hide away in some foreign land,' was gouged over with *It pants for your arrival.* Now, looking at Esp on his stage, I thought the man's criticisms graceless and mean. I remembered Esp's explanation of 'contraband', his sideways comments on 'Headey scribblers', the man's beloved greats of literature. It would have made no difference if Esp had tried, improbably, to placate him by copying them. If he'd got in a fustian tizzy about a skylark, a russet autumn he'd never seen, the red ink would still have flowed. Right now, though, that didn't matter. 'If You Don't Love Me'? What wasn't to love about the boy? Under the grinding fans in our flung-windowed room, he was monumental.

And here he came again. This time through, the greats traded places: passion and heartbreak were differently shuffled. Otis Redding supplied the footwork, Sam Cooke and—yes, even the Marley for whom he professed indifference—shared duties in the second verse. The Big O was just striding in again for that jewel of a finale when Headey's shadow fell hard and wide. Esp looked at the hand on his arm. Blowing invisible locks from his face, setting his jaw like Engelbert Humperdinck (where the hell had he come from?), he raised his eyes, locked them onto Headey's:

'Aw, you love it. Ain't you love it all along? You need this Voice of Grenada huge-time.' The punch landed square on Headey's chest. We exploded.

The fallout was Biblical. Headey's gaze swept the room, swept again, his eyes so crazed that I expected red ink to jet out of them. He lingered with particular malice on Eric, who'd naturally exploded with the rest of us.

Then, *phhht!* teacher and headliner were gone. Through the doorway we had a glimpse of Headey leaning hard away like a pyramid-jockey with an obstinate slab. His back-stretched hand didn't seem to know where it gripped Esp, but the boy's protesting voice—deserted now by Redding, Orbison, Cooke—told how hard and uncaring the grip was. The irregular clatter of doors took them further, further off. We stared at each other.

And waited. The fans creaked. Beyond the windows, voices and stray engines went about their business. One minute...five. For sure Headey had detonated before, but this was gigantic. Then again, no one in his custody had ever landed a blow on that unlovely frame. Five...ten. I was hoping—maybe we all were—that humanity would win out: that Headey was just keeping Esp pinned to a wall while he had an all-out glower; that Esp would come springing through the door, a bit of twinkle-dust still on him, followed by Headey and his oldest routine, finger-wags and syllables in lock-step, reminding Esp and all of us of stan-dards, co-mmit-ment, fo-cus—esp. focus. The man's face might give Jove the frits but at least he'd be saying stuff.

Then we were spilling into the corridor. At first, the invisible ropes of school-hood kept us from going further. Hanging on the door frame, Twinko looked far down the way Headey and Esp had gone, then back the other way. We understood. It was an uncontested fact that, when the school was built, Headey had sat smack dab in the middle of the site—the breathing centre, milord amid his schemes—and the whole place had gone up around him. He was the place, had been rumoured to walk through its walls. He might drag Esp back from any-old-where—down through the ceiling wouldn't surprise.

At last, Eric padded off, Twinko swung down behind him and we all followed. He pushed open the first swing-door, and noise jittered in from different rooms. A high voice recited the principal somethings of Guatemala. Another, surely Flutter Priestman's, despaired of a broken-backed scale on a piano: 'What's that? No, that there, under your index. B sharp? You go invent B sharp?' 'Straight, I want,' came barking from our left. 'Straight lines, two of them…. What? Well, move it'— and a table whined across a floor.

'Shit.' Eric. Eric who never swore. He had the next swing-door ajar with his knee. We bundled around him: 'Quiet,' said his down-pushing hand. 'Listen.'

Behind us, the high voice was giving Panama the topographic once-over, the piano was walloping out 'Chopsticks' (more Priestman snidery, no doubt), the barker was hup-hup-hupping. Eric said 'There!' and all sounds vanished, routed by a long bellow of pain.

We were pushing through the door when the barker jumped us.

'What arc all you about?'

Another bellow answered. The barker—Mr Rohan, a sports instructor new that term—got ahead of Eric and Twinko and, shading his eyes, peered down the corridor. There could have been more pain, but Priestman drowned it with a fist on the keys. Troubled, Mr Rohan gestured us to retreat. Eric and Twinko stood sentinel by our door till the bell went. Beyond, in the school and the

21

world, all was muffled now. We kept an effortful silence, congregants struggling and failing to find a prayer for present need. Only Twinko broke it:

'How you making out with Ambrose guitar?'

Not bad, nodded Eric, not bad. Again we fell to our fruitless praying.

At the end of the afternoon we waited down the road, among the trees by Duttine's Cooler. Usually, Duttine got serious business out of us: 'Man, allyuh should sign with Pepsi direct,' he'd more than once advised.[10] 'Leave me 'nuff for general clients.' This time, though, we left the bottles and shakes untouched. Under the trees we slumped, our bodies singing with Duttine's generator while, between visits by the general clients, he squinted across at us like a puzzled doctor:

'Plug of ice? Pallet?[11] On the house?' He slapped his awning. No one answered.

At last, something came out of the heat. We rose, started forward and hung irresolute. It was like a desert scene in a movie: for an age, you can't tell if what you see is a living form or a trick of the shimmer. But then enough dark and depth came together to prove our eyes right. We walked to meet him.

The shoulders swung a bit, then went limp. The knees jellied, stiffened, jellied again—once so bad that Twinko and I leapt forward, arms gathering air. This was pop nightmare: the Big O with stage fright, Michael Jackson clueless in mid-swivel. The eyes were as dull as a man's

---

[10] Allyuh: all of you people.

[11] Ice lolly.

last hour. Headey had caught him royal.[12]

Twinko grabbed him by the shoulders: 'Man, we'll carry this news to St George's. He won't give no person more the red ink.'

Esp shook his head, pressed a finger to Twinko's mouth, withdrew it, stroked the wing of his nose:

'He know what I got. He don't like liking it, but what he do? I put a spell on the man. He give me big bacchanal'—he closed his eyes in weird bliss—'like fan mail.'[13]

I stared hard at him. He didn't look like he'd put anything on anyone. All but lifeless, he could have been miming Headey's soul in some dangerous charade. Astonishment at 'Purple Haze'? Breathlessness at the grand-standing close to 'In Dreams'? Love of rolling 'contraband' round his mouth, of making those noises melt together again and again? His very being denied that such wonders had ever found him.

'It's just his way,' he whispered then, seeming to speak out of a maturity that shouldn't have been his, ours, not yet, and for sure had eluded Headey. What could you do with that? Nothing, there was no time, our hands were all over him, breaking his collapse in the road. We got him sat down. As if now charading a caterpillar, he hunkered tight, knees drawn up, hands crowning bowed head. Eric squatted, rested a hand on his shoulder. Twinko and I checked him over. No marks, or none we could see. Well, the likes of Headey, they worked close,

---

[12] Given him hell.

[13] Bacchanal: serious quarrel, confusion.

close. I remembered Esp's cheery destruction of Sean Connery the day we were set the free composition: *'You want me to talk, Mr Headey? No, Mr Bond, I want you to siiing.'* Well, he had. And somewhere in Headey's ineffable mind, a villain to end them all had sat immobile save for desultory strokes of a white cat; had smiled, bided— peeled away time like you'd strip a bug of its legs and wings, till he found his moment. If that was fandom...

'You fella had fuss with a boobooman?'[14] called Duttine. 'Or what he at?'

Twinko pushed away from the group: 'I'll get him a Pepper. Shut the old one up.'

---

[14] A ghost.

4

The Rock Exponents weren't long for this world. They puttered on, even got some yard-gigs in Harford, Grenville, faraway Felix Park. Eric and Twinko weren't just doing it because they felt sorry for Esp. They wanted to make music, and both, by now, were pretty handy. But more, they wanted Esp to get back what had been thundered out of him that afternoon. And, yes, he wrote more songs, yes, the Big O and James Brown crept tentatively back towards that rangy body. At Twinko's suggestion, they called themselves the 'Ponents, this being the only salvageable bit of the original; to everyone's surprise, Esp deemed it cool. But so much had been lost. His songs were just more collisions between boy and girl, one-verse notions stretched thinner than thin. The gigs were loose-limbed affairs stuffed with call-and-response. We had a great time at them, but it was the kind of great you mainly generate yourself. I mean, even with the hole in Esp's heart, the 'Ponents were sound enough, but it would have taken someone tragic, a ruff-shirted loser with nothing to offer but 'Puff, the Magic Dragon', to destroy the vibe. If there was another foreign land lurking in Esp's head, more contraband, he never sang them. His music and life were off their pace.

Yet here and there, the old glory broke through. Just before one number in the set, Esp would swing up the neck of his guitar, Eric and Twinko would exchange looks and all was riot. It would be some old warhorse, 'Johnny B. Goode' or 'My Girl', but it was as if the old Esp, arriving late and breathless, had pushed through the crowd, split the skin of the onstage Esp, leapt in and proceeded to give it nails. Throughout the song, whatever way he was twitching and sliding, Esp kept his eyes focused like a madman on a spot beyond the crowd. It was as if, Eric surmised, he'd spotted Headey, in attendance heaven knows why, and was determined to booglarise his number one fan-in-denial. The song would end, and he'd slip back down through the gears. Perhaps, once again, the phantom Headey had shaken his head—*Not this time either, Mr Belmar*—and dissolved into the bougainvillea night. Perhaps it was this repeated thumbs-down from the spectre among the trees that finally made him give his fellow 'Ponents their cards.

Whether Headey was carpeted or not, we never knew. If Esp knew, he didn't say. Not, was our guess—otherwise, surely the old Esp would have risen again, capering about in the glow of vindication. Or maybe swift vindication had less to do with it than we supposed. As Eric uneasily suggested, and we uneasily saw the sense of, maybe Esp would have regarded rescue by a third party—Principal Tutela, ears jetting steam, giving Headey the big what-for—as an admission that he couldn't fight his own battles…more, as an interruption in some intense rite of passage. Esp had failed the first bout. Or had he? Perhaps he saw it as a draw. Why else, if Eric's surmise held water, had he stared so fervently into the dark beyond the yard-parties? By that reckoning, he still figured he had Headey on a string, helplessly drawn to something that stood for all the man loathed in the culture that surrounded him, hemmed him in, thumbed its nose at Keats and Austen fooling round by the ha-ha.

Of course, a few brisk questions to Esp might have cleared it up. But we were at an age to thirst for drama. For sure, Headey sacked or busted down to stationery-jockey—that would have been satisfying, but it would have meant a neat end to the whole kalinda.[15] Some continuation, shifting and vague, of the kind which Eric claimed to see in Esp's brooding eyes, was more like it. Plus, we took excitedly to the idea of Eric as Esp's shaman, divining the whirlpools in the broken hero's mind. Naturally, being who he was, Eric never got theatrical: claimed his musings were exactly that. But he had no jurisdiction over how we'd pick them up. The Voice of Grenada, shaken bad but, deep down where we couldn't see, already regrouping—that, too, was rock 'n' roll.

Mr Rohan, the barker in the corridor, played his part. Or obliviously played the part we handed him. A rumour got up about how he hadn't settled for looking anxious, ordering us away. We already had him pegged as a freedom-fighter on uneasy terms with his contract. Now there were sightings of him staring aghast at Headey, hanging round outside Principal Tutela's office. Whatever long game Esp was or wasn't playing, Mr Rohan wanted action on his behalf now. Robbie Watts, one of our crowd and not particularly given to reflection, observed once that the young sports instructor looked a bit like Sidney Poitier. That was perfect: Mr Rohan morphed instantly from basketball-thumper to icon of justice. It didn't take a whole spread of time for 'a bit like'

---

[15] Literally, stick-fight.

to become 'rather…very much…amazingly'. That nothing came of his unverifiable efforts played nicely into the Esp saga. Even a figure of evident (if modest) authority was swept aside by The Man. That Mr Rohan had been offered a Head of Sports job in Port of Spain and was doorstepping the Principal about breaking his contract—not to mention giving Headey dirty looks because the latter had accused him of dishonour in a Staff meeting—only emerged later, when he simply didn't reappear after Corpus Christi.[16] No matter. He'd earned his role—walk-on but riveting—in the whole affair. As remarked by Twinko, who soon fancied himself a diviner in the Eric mould, we weren't meant to find out till way afterwards—and hell, the sports instructor *had* looked daggers at Headey. That on its own put him on some plinth in Esp's vicinity: one of the Four Tops, a Temptation. Who cared about reality?

'Bon Jay, what is reality?' Twinko enquired of the tiring sky on a walk home one night. That shut us up, though Eric gave him a *how long you got?* look. Suspecting that he'd overreached, Twinko just executed brisk funk on a passing fence.

One thing we saw with our own eyes, though, was how Headey behaved during the rest of our time with him. Besting Esp, it seemed, had taken its toll. Something niggled him. Going more ape-shit than he should have that day? Belatedly deciding that Esp's old-pals punch hadn't been worth his wrath and fire? Heaven forbid that anything like teacher-student morality figured in his

---

[16] 7th June, a public holiday.

thinking. It was no good pumping my father for insights: his occasional collisions with Headey were for drink, not talk. Whatever, the man couldn't quite look the boy in the eye. Esp's compositions came back with the usual red violation of his blocky writing, but Headey made less of a to-do—and soon, no to-do at all—about their quality. He even handed them back to Esp with a weird courtesy, like a trainee mailman. For his part Esp smiled in quiet content, as though he'd earned—no, been gifted—the right to flay English alive. Headey's all-purpose bluster hit its old peaks, sure it did, but the performance was effortful, a touch comic. Never again was he as happily baronial with us. Once, during a silent comprehension, I gazed up at him. He was edged back into a corner of the room, hitherto alien space for him, looking like he was fighting a fart in church.

5

Soon enough we were gone. Some of us shed the beauties and encumbrances of Harford, Soubise, Union Village for the bigger elsewhere: St George's, Grenville, even—dizzyingly—Port of Spain or Kingston. Others got work on home turf, bartending and odd-jobbing at one or several of the swank hotels mushrooming in the Harford area, whose names were heavy on 'Blue', 'Bliss', 'Ocean'. These were the home-birds, family guys in training, going steady or pretty damn close. I admired their certainty about the track of their lives. Forests, stores, faces known forever—these were inexhaustible to them. They were believers without the compulsion to spread the word. Really, I envied them and in some ways still do.

Twinko made out OK. His stint as 'Ponents drummer led to hired-gun work, sitting in when some band's guy was indisposed for colourful reasons. Finally he worked a split-shift between an outfit in Grenville and one in Upper Capital. Both were big on Marley, Toots, Sly and Robbie, our own Eddie Bullen and David Emmanuel—all much more to the point, for Twinko, than Elvis or the Big O, even when they scraped the sky.

An Economics scholarship led to Eric's dazzling Germany—well, Bonn—with his shamanic hold over numbers. Word was that he'd become pretty fleet on guitar. More, he'd learned German in a week and was set fair for Danish and Dutch. I couldn't help thinking of the play that had broken Headey down on that dark afternoon. Now, effortlessly, Eric was a conquistador of the tongue. And he was one of a small bunch of us who gave new time zones a try. Some went to the US,

30

practically dragged through the doors of colleges in a country which, perhaps, now felt a bit bad about its Grenadian stopover in '83. After written and phoned interventions by Principal Tutela, proof of funds secured by church drives, I got a part-scholarship in less contentious Canada.

Esp vanished.

It was in Canada, I guess, that I began to feel the creep of admiration for those home-birds. I wouldn't call it homesickness: you need a copper-bottomed sense of home to get that, and even then I was beginning to realize that there was more of the tumbleweed in me than I might have thought. It was more a weird vulnerability. As I said at the start, I love the voices that come from home, the sheer fact of the journey they make—all those gum-sealed words migrating on cross-continent thermals. But as my first autumn in Canada wore on, and the letters started coming, I felt a growing powerlessness. I was here, the doings of home—some predictable, others a surprise—were rooted there. My mind, it seemed, wasn't big enough to accommodate the here-and-thereness of it all. I could maybe take refuge in a confident word like displacement. But Harford and all Grenada were starting to lose purchase in my mind, and the bracing pastoral of Nova Scotia was yet to take whatever charge it would. Like home, place is something you need big dollops of certainty about before you can feel as diasporic as some people seem to manage. Sometimes, having read the latest letter, I'd head out through the nearer parts of the Annapolis Valley—the dyke-trails round the Minas Basin, the Cornwallis River paths—and plant my feet hard to feel the thump of the land all through me. The ambush of new seasons made the strange stranger. The colours of the Annapolis Valley, the provincial ridges and uplands, the downright mountains—they were not so very different, maybe, from stretches of my home island; but as the year approached its end, they sent up their cries: *northern, northern, bundle up, your own body has to create whatever of that old forsaken sun you can get next to your heart.* Then the snow flew. Even before then, though, the pages from home seemed more and more like tidings from a planet which figured in a recurring dream. For some reason, the absence of any reference to Esp deepened the unreality.

Mom was the main correspondent, doing an occasional turn-and-turn-about with Uncle Padmore. Surprisingly, Robbie Watts—the faint peripheral in our group, whose sole achievement was to twin Mr Rohan with Sidney Poitier—joined in too, establishing himself in my mind as home-bird-in-chief. Or perhaps not so surprising: since Canada, since telling off my subsequent months in England, I've come to see that some connections with old lives aren't faint but pending, freed at last to strengthen when old contexts, old pecking-orders, have gone. Robbie was doing all right, had a girl, was working at *La Galaxie Bleue,* one of the new hotels in the Harford area. He was a handy correspondent, too, which shouldn't have surprised me. His efforts for Headey never survived assault, not like Eric's play, but they got out half-alive. He came into his own in a way he never had when we'd all hung round the school steps or Duttine's Cooler or Esp's yard-gigs. Perhaps he'd found his own gig now we'd scattered—a gatekeeper, ushering past, present and future in and out. He was certainly tireless, evidently keeping up with Eric and Twinko, passing on their news, promising to relay mine: a good and bad thing, this, since it played to my laziness, sapped my resolve to write them direct. One beguiling bit of Robbie's letters was the sense they conveyed, through recaps or asides, that he'd wanted their quality to be better than it turned out. He needn't have worried. He taught me lots.

Sometime round my first Christmas in Nova Scotia, Esp started to reappear like a ship in the far offing. One of my mom's family and neighbourhood round-ups ended with 'Some or other body saw that piece of foolery Belmar up Sauteurs way, Carib's Leap they said, isn't that like him to fix on a leaping place?' Robbie confirmed this, adding that he must have dropped south thereafter: 'He was spotted in Victoria striding along the street, loaf of bread in one hand, guitar in the other. My guess was he'd been Grenadines way. But Twinko's Ambrose said he saw some kid acting pure crazy in Caracas, the East Park. Singing, whooping, spinning, playing mad flamenco on guitar. He hasn't seen Esp for years but he told Twinko about it when he was last home. "That's him," says our Twinko, "that's our Voice." We could ask the Belmars, only we can't. You see them around but they have a look in their eyes—"We don't know or we won't say. You choose." Maybe I sound mad, but this piecing it all together is more fun than downright fact.'

He was right, and what he said reminded me of our speculations on whether Headey was ever brought to book for his vileness, whether Mr Rohan really did step up to the plate for Esp. Robbie, me, Twinko, maybe Eric too: a little troupe of Sam Spades, Miss Marples without the high teas and leaded windows, linking this scrap to that, standing back, stroking our chins. My image of Esp took on an almost spiritual cast. He seemed like the subject of one of those church banners you see through Advent: *He is coming…He is coming…He is here.* As the Annapolis snow fell and other students greeted me with 'Cold enough for ya?', I almost felt a niggly disappointment that, at some point, he might be.

But the clues kept coming, kept forcing Miss Marple to set down her buttered scone. Now we got into the Case of the Phantom Postcard. Mom said she'd heard—from 'some or other body', her usual careful trope for informants—that 'fool Belmar' was asking for my address, and this she'd duly passed on. Nothing arrived. In her next letter, she appeared to quote from another some or other body acting on Esp's behalf, hoping I'd got his postcard. 'Don't hold a morsel of breath, Henderson,' she added, 'he won't know to buy or write a card, dream he lives in.' I wrote care of his folks saying sorry, I got no card, but how's things? Silence. Then it was Robbie, putting flesh on the some or other body as 'this guy round Harford' who'd come into *La Galaxie Bleue*, asked if Robbie knew me and repeated Esp's enquiry about the card. A while later, with a Job-like patience she hadn't always shown at home, Mom took her turn, saying that her some or other body had again been approached, reiterating Esp's supposed anxiety. Her sense of duty stopped right there: 'Forget it, honey—

boy like him too chupid not to lick stamps both side.' No one could sigh words across a page like her.

By this time, my winter fastness was getting nicely warmed by the image of all those some or other bodies, relays of them, cantering up and down from Sauteurs to True Blue Bay and back, grabbing Cokes or beers from the drink-stands spread round the island, conferring about the swelling corpus of Esp's work that simply wasn't reaching me. Postcards, schmostcards—what of the lyrics, the stories—the meditations on Headey?

The question of whether our old English teacher still squatted in Esp's heart came and went in my mind, and it was nudged into relief by a curious letter from Uncle Padmore. By this time other students, profs, storekeepers were assuring me that spring was just round the corner: a wickedly slothful corner, it seemed. And there'd been fresh sightings. The link-man for one of the 'Ponents' last gigs was sure as sure Esp had spent a night in Clabony. A lone figure had been spotted round Seven Sisters Waterfalls by a Harford local ('singing the clouds away,' Robbie lyrically reported, 'about foreign lands, contrabands—who else could it be?'). One morning, the proprietor of 'Daddy Hands' restaurant at Brandon Hall had chased a sleepy troubadour from his stoop, receiving 'What Becomes of the Broken-Hearted?' for his pains from the back-end of the village.

Uncle Padmore confirmed this last in his letter, which was otherwise void of news. That was him all over: cut straight to meditations, abstractions, the big picture. News of my village, my siblings—one of whom was now caught in Headey's net—could be left to Mom. Headey, in fact, was now his embedded text, with Esp hovering by. Inevitably, Uncle Padmore was not a fan of the sporadic booziness that connected the teacher to my father: 'What my brother-in-law your father thinks he's doing, I have no idea. Why he plays Igor to that ba-john's Frankenstein—here, Henderson, I hold up my hands and I let them fall.'[17] In Uncle Padmore's conversation and writings, Dad was always 'my brother-in-law your father', a double-status that, echoing 'My Mother…The Queen Mother', ennobled him as nothing else had or would. 'But you're a college-man now,' Uncle went on, 'and, while I didn't give you my best belt or *Les Paul And Mary Ford Live With The Dixie Hummingbirds* as a parting gift, perhaps I can fix that omission through discourse.'

This wasn't a new wheeze. In the past couple of years, I'd been fed many of Uncle's discourses. Invariably, they'd meant reminiscences of his time in England. Like an Aesop fable without the kick, they lacked a definable purpose—unless I was meant to understand that, as the older boy in the family, I would in time be assuming a mantle that his brother-in-law my father wasn't aware he'd got on and I thus needed tipping off about the world's doings. The world he spoke of at such times was a zillion miles from anything I knew: cramped, smoky, like a rackety engine room at the corner of a factory yard; surveyed from on high, through plate glass windows, by the top brass—those, in fact, who had managed us till 1974, gifting sizeable chunks of legacy, any one of which would have made a perfect sequel for Eric's history play.

---

[17] Ba-john: a bully, a mean customer.

Uncle stuck names on this belching world: Smethwick, Winson Green, Tyseley, Old Hill, Bilston, Wolverhampton Low Level. This last fascinated me. While I accepted Uncle's explanation—two stations side by side, High Level for people, Low for freight—it struck me as a name from some imperial reworking of Genesis, in which, like snakes banished to drag about on their bellies, certain towns had to face the world with their morality spelt out.

It was hard to imagine Uncle in those places: Uncle with his command of words and figures—not far off Eric's, I thought—and now…well, maybe not top clerk in Grenada but pretty damn close. But 'needs must, must, must' as he'd say on a rising note. And back in his day, the need was for him to earn elsewhere and send money home—as, in a comfier way, I was being bred to do. He'd joke about his belated migration to England: 'They put me in a dinghy rear of *Windrush*. The binding rope was eighteen years long.' So, he was a warehouse-jack, a freight-heaver, a fiddler with bolts and brackets as they swanned past on assembly lines. He'd been called King Kong in his time. He'd been dispatched to ask for a sky-blue, dog-leg screwdriver.

It was that last job—at a gas appliance factory near Roseville, a settlement that ribboned the Birmingham-Wolverhampton road—to which he returned for his present discourse. The late Sixties it was—flowers, 'I Was Kaiser Bill's Batman', happenings in the sunlit south of England. None of this touched Roseville. But Headey did…or rather, Arthur Nettleton. This fable had its proper kick.

Nettleton was the foreman with special responsibility for the cookers: a responsibility that grew hawk's eyes once he'd located Uncle's whereabouts on the line. Like Death in a morality play, calling time at any old hour, he would swoop on Uncle: 'Check how that grill's seated…well, check it again, then…that's gonna bloody jam, that handle…what you done with them nuts? Finger-tight, I said, finger-tight. Some poor bugger's gonna waste a day trying get them loose. God A'mighty, Padmore, come down from your bloody tree.'

The white men and women on the lines got much the same treatment from Nettleton. Even if all was flowing smoothly, some weird chagrin often moved him to bawl out the chargehands. But the whites could give it back in his words, his accent, so that—to Uncle—they seemed to be having a family flame-up rather than plotting his destruction. Then, Nettleton would take a step back, flip up his hands like Mr Astonished in a melodrama:

'Here, rear, rear, rear—I'm obliged to honour my remit, pal. I'm in the way of being answerable. And I don't want'—here he would often draw his finger across his throat, supposedly reminding them that he'd have to take the fall for any shoddiness. Since this was devoutly wished, his performance invariably got a whistle or a round of applause, at which point he would retreat in a burst of oaths, as an *artiste* might cry 'Troglodytes!' when pelted offstage.

'You would not believe this man,' wrote Uncle. 'If the line broke, was it our fault? Who would blame us for exchanging a word or two? Getting settled with the newspaper? But no—back Master Death comes striding, oathing the chargehands, blasting his gun.'

Bob Garrett hadn't stood for it: had tired of even arguing the toss with Nettleton. He'd brought one square-off to a tidy end by sending Nettleton 'crown over fundament', as Uncle put it, across a pallet stacked with completed eye-level grills:

'Tens of scores of damage. A gang of suits came running down—first time they'd seen the shop floor. Poor Bob was egressed on the spot'—and elevated to people's hero. Thereafter, Nettleton lost momentum. He still huffed and created, but it only needed some of the women to start singing 'We wanna be Bobby's girls, we wanna be…' to spike his routine.

'Do you see, Henderson, how I'm connecting here? Can you see Nettleton, can you hear him? Of course you can. You saw him, heard him up and down your line in the English room. "Man, I've got a remit—Man, I'm answerable." Two specimens of jobsworth, boy: acqui full of ink,[18] boss-man with pocket stuff-full of pens and him with no clue past "A is for Apple". Jobsworth, I say.'

And he did, again, and explained it. For me, the word was up there with Eric's 'swart', and I wished I'd known it back in the English room. I imagined spreading it, all of us barking it that afternoon as Headey closed on Esp. Confused, 'torrentialised' as Uncle would say, he loosed his grip on the Voice of Grenada and took off, lone and howling, down the corridor. Except, of course, he didn't. Then again, it was easy to picture a lone, howling Nettleton among the battered grills. The Headey we'd

---

[18] Acqui: a teacher.

watched in the weeks after his dismantling of Esp hadn't perhaps been so very different. Bold or cowed, though, he'd still been doing something to Esp's mind. Was he still?

'I feel sorry for that boy,' said Uncle Padmore, 'but then I would.' Well, he would. He'd fed Esp the sounds that enthralled him, led him to punch Headey and totter at hell's mouth. But that meant we were all in it: I passed the sounds on to Esp, no one blocked his embrace of madness that afternoon. But thinking like that, you could drown yourself in the round-and-round. Uncle wasn't to blame. Eric had insisted that his shaman-turn with Esp's mind was pure speculation—but we boys still tore into it like scripture. How was Uncle to know what groves of peril awaited Esp beyond Les and Mary? How were Les and Mary to know? '*Helter-Skelter*,' confessed Charles Manson. 'That was my killing-theme.' Music, eh? Any three-minute song could heal the world or burst its balloon. It depends who hears. Like a Headey.

Meantime, though, there was another lesson in Uncle's protracted sign-off:

'Jobsworths, my boy, they're everywhere. They hide in the trash. No self-dignifying roof would give them sleep. If you're a whisker late through the door, they rip off an hour's pay like a suit-sleeve. If your tyre's a fairy-kiss away from the yellow line, they're all over the windshield with their bills of condemnation. Keep your eyes peeled, Henderson—the eyes in your eyes the same. The Wazzock of Roseville, they called him.' ('Wazzock' was another gloss, another nifty word for me to tuck away.) 'Just imagine, Henderson, handing that on your dispatch-card to St Peter. Nettleton is legion, boy, a pork-faced Beelzebub. If there's a permit to void, he's a-voiding. If there's some widow to catch royal because her dead one didn't square the last payment on his boots, boy, her front door will rattle into the witch-hours. If there's a way to stop your sky's blue, your fire's heat, Nettleton will be alongside you, casting his shadow like a shroud. No more splashing in the happy lake for you. And your jobsworth, he'll do this mock-gentleman thing, call you stuff like "My friend" and "Chief". What is that, Chief? He got some Lone Ranger thing going? He a Son of the Pioneers? Jobsworths, boy. Always and everywhere, taking up blessed space to spite the constituency.'

Songs are diaries. And letters are diary entries that someone else has thoughtfully given you to slip among your own loose leaves. I can remember exactly when and where I read and re-read Uncle's letter. Spring exams were just done (and spring had properly arrived to support their designation). I was in a café in Port Maitland, bearing onto the Gulf of Maine. Facing me was Ian Paskin, a contemporary, the son of a prof whose roots were in Northampton. Behind me was a huge, beam-strung flag of Nova Scotia, which, though we were as far from the door as possible, stirred at every scrap of air, occasionally brushing my shoulder as though I'd turned a page too fast for its attention. I read the Nettleton and jobsworth bits out loud. Though I didn't doubt Uncle's account, I was happy to have Ian corroborate, from his own family history, its general drift and atmosphere. His dad was of garage-owning stock, Corby and, later on, Wolverhampton. Yes, the place-names were spot-on; yes, his dad's early world had taken in yards and depots and dust. British Steel, he added, had twinned Corby with Bilston in a singular celebration: the plants in both places had closed within weeks of each other.

I think he must have gone hunting the waitress for more coffee then. At any rate, I was alone, and the names Uncle had gifted me began swirling their smoke around my head. Each place picked out a song, a singer: an Exponents or 'Ponents number, or from Uncle's treasury of sound or out of the spangly pop-music blue that had wrapped round my home years. Elvis was all shook up at Wolverhampton Low Level, possibly from the shunt-yard's racket. Marley asked a woman on the cooker line if she could be loved, before Nettleton hugely intervened, insisting that he scarper to his banana boat. Big O walked in dreams, talked in them to no one in particular, except for the huge, soot-winged birds which, I imagined, terrorised Winson Green from the rooflines. Esp was everywhere: *I'll hide away in some foreign land,* he pleaded, heart breaking, to the streaks of dismal cloud that flowed radially from Birmingham, *where nobody can contraband.* My suspension between here and there, my neither-ness, expanded. Places I'd felt with heart and eye embroiled themselves with the names in the custody of Uncle's neat hand. When Ian returned, I shouldn't have been surprised to see him transformed into Sam Cooke, Mr Rohan, the big O, Nettleton, Headey or Garrett the revenger.

A day or so later, Robbie got me back on track: 'He's here. I've heard all about him.'

6

The hotels around Harford Village stand this way and that on the island's eastern side. They are what they are meant to be: dream-harbours, consoling and inspiring the guest after their year-long trudge through work and bills. Photographed, they lie their cool rooflines against untroubled blue. Awnings and verandahs are matters of style as much as of practicality. Trees lean into the photos, trim and muscular, reminding the viewer that they, too, have figured in their dreams. The hotels around Harford Village could be anywhere uncomplicatedly hot and desirable. Like their doubles on other soft coasts, they whisper to the east, west, south—and especially north—of wave and sail, palms that fringe obligingly, tonics for young bones, romance of unguessable nature and outcome.

The hotels around Harford Village have many voices. England chirps. France and the Teuton belt give poised accounts of themselves. Scandinavia murmurs, Spain comes and goes via South American couriers, Italy can't help itself. Mandarin waxes, Hindi is not unheard. Fronting them all, though, is the choppiness of New York, the laze of the Carolinas, the Middle West's open-necked broadness, Pacific California's buzz of promised lands and deal-closure.

Knowing the caprices of the external world, the hoteliers work hard on domesticity. Truculent winds can scupper a day's sailing; marine life can simply clear off, uniqueness and all; determined rain can turn an excursion through the island's Four Parishes into the tourist's memory of a weepy Monday morning on a northern rat run. Under hotel roofs, though, the mood stays constant. Staff are quietly efficient, food is punctual, a coaster slides beneath each drink. Music, too, is hospitality's version of art that conceals art. Genres are carefully scheduled, bands and singers imprinting different sounds on different nights. Tonight it's the smoother end of jazz, tomorrow a reggae whose polemics are filed down. At other times there is an unfocussed nod to the Caribbean's notional ways of work and leisure, with ditties about fishing nets and cut cane, the consumption of rum to quench thirst, molten sunsets dropping like a stone, each with choruses of anthemic easiness.

This isn't to say that the experimental is unknown. Chinese pianists have been heard singing 'By The Time I Get To Phoenix'. But there is much emphasis on tickling the fancies of patrons who are, perhaps, flush and unfulfilled at the same time. So an audience may hear of a yesterday with trouble far away (when you, executive from Twickenham, were fancy-free, unsaddled with an astringent wife, teenagers who say 'whatever' a lot and insist you promised them Jamaica). Or of this guy in love with you (lone woman from Westchester, needing the sun on your face rather than the spittle of a man you've begun to divorce). Or of this island in the sun, yet another gift from the Father's hand (and, after singing that, how could you not love it, designer from Oslo, peculiar though it might be alongside the fur-haloed hurry of your home?). Sometimes, of course, a voice sings of the end being near, facing the final curtain, but that's the catharsis spot, nicely judged, deep in the evening and booze. For each such moment, there's a yellow ribbon. For each regret, there's an old oak tree. Nothing is unpredictable, nothing is wacky. A lone, dishevelled songster with unproven repertoire would be shown the terrace exit.

Whole communities can be decanted into hotel service. By the time I left for Canada, a good half of my family were scrubbing or bellhopping in one be-flagged fantasy or another. This was indenture for our times: not only did employees sign contracts, they also got to use their initials over and over, affirming that facilities had been checked at ten and would be again at twelve. But these weren't the swart plantation miles of Eric's fancy. Though they privately plumed themselves on some kind of superiority, the management didn't turn a vinous, patrician eye upon their workers. A bullish manager, a regular ba-john, could find himself in the unquiet lands of folklore, his establishment quickly unstaffed as if, overnight, it had become a site of curses. Work was important but arseness, intolerable. Arthur Nettleton would have had a hard time keeping so much as a luggage-jockey in his employ. Knowing all this, management trod carefully and also invited locals to enjoy their bars, their lounges, seeing this as both an endorsement and a way of putting guests at their ease so they wouldn't go home defining Grenadians purely as guides, cab-men, serfs of the modern world. And if said locals had some status, so much the better. Managers could nod respectfully at them. They could make a big to-do of entering lobbies as though about to buy the place on a whim. Proprietorially comfy among the transients, they were half-personage, half-'character'.

Headey became known as one such. For all his militant aestheticism in school, he loved his comforts outside it, treasuring especially their public dimension. Shack-bars and Duttine's Cooler simply wouldn't do. Comfort and largesse—initially his but ideally everyone else's—were the thing. On fan-stroked verandahs, in airy lounges, creditworthy tongues of all nations around him, he would hold court with compadres old and new. (My father was excluded from these occasions and didn't press to join. Whether this was through spoken or unspoken agreement, I never knew. But Headey would slum it in dark corners whenever he and my father had bottles to scare. Perhaps Mom had counselled my father—using the words of some or other body—that, bad though these encounters were, overt fraternisation was worse. Perhaps Uncle Padmore had offered discursive words to his brother-in-law, including the tale of Nettleton. I didn't probe. If Headey chose shadows in which to give my frailly charming father some of his brutish time, that was the best of a bad job.)

In the same letter in which he'd said Esp was back, Robbie mentioned cashing up late one night when he spotted Headey walking up and down outside *La Galaxie Bleue*. His face had its customary fierceness, flaring competitively with the front lights. Next morning he was back again, as if it were his purpose to examine the place under every angle of sun and moon. Robbie crept across to some lounge foliage and peered out. Headey walked off beyond the jutting lobby, along by the ground-floor rooms, turned and came back, rocked on his heels, stroked his chin. It would have been no wonder, said

Robbie, if he'd started on that thumb-twisting business that landscape artists do:

'He's never been in here. Checking whether we're his fit, maybe.'

Looking back now, I remember a sad fancy settling on me: imagined that he was checking the lobby roof to see if it would bear my father's weight and, if so, whether he intended to plonk him up there already drunk for foreign astonishment, a local of especially startling aspect.

I'd barely had time to digest this letter when Robbie sent another. By now my replies were chaotically out of sequence and, as often before, I wondered if he had, or cared to give, any time to anything else in his life. He'd mentioned that he was sending much the same reports to Eric in Bonn. What did his family have to say about his priorities? What did his girl think? Did he work his *Galaxie Bleue* shifts quick-quick and then, as other writers had romantically done, hole up in some cupboard and write the way you'd breathe? Then again, this turnaround was sharpish even for him, and I soon saw why.

His informants—whose dedication and strength of number clearly rivalled my mother's—had breathlessly got back to him. Esp had hit the ground running. His sighting in Harford was, mused Robbie, brief but powerful publicity, as of a placard-man running full tilt down the street. He was now 'Your Nowherian',[19] a disarming mix of generosity and allusion to his months off the map. I imagined it writ large on every vulnerable wall in that blocky hand of his. In no time, he'd done solo

---

[19] A person of no fixed abode.

floor-spots in Grenville, gigs with popular bands and shouters, an all-nighter at St George's. Kamille, a waitress at *La Galaxie Bleue* and stalwart at 'Ponents' yard-gigs, had seen him in action. Robbie gave her words as light a touch as he could. Esp's days in the wilderness, it seemed, had created a leaven of chaos and discipline.

On the one hand, his swivel was back, his guitar again joyful. Delighted folks in Grenville heard him say 'Yeah' and threw it back at him. But this wasn't just for a one-song explosion in the old yard-gig repertoire. Sam, Elvis, the Big O were alongside him for much of the time. He'd written new songs—pretty damn good, Kamille said—including a riposte to his own 'If You Don't Love Me', seemingly all sparks and combustion, in which the singer declared that he was off to see the world in the morning and his girl could like or lump it:

'"I'll Show You Good, Sister", that one is,' reported Robbie, 'and he tells his craft if she don't like, he won't spin her no more in his multi-colour dream.[20] Kamille remembered that last bit specially. Don't ask what it means.' I was happy not to. But it sounded like he'd moved on from contraband, from asking one fragile word to be everything and nothing.

On the other hand—maybe in Caracas, the Grenadines, on Pluto—he'd apparently learned to work the crowd like a real pro. He knew when to tone it down—arguably because, at last, he'd listened to Sam, Otis and the rest telling him that, hey, power wasn't all about top gear. Kamille had enthused about a new

---

[20] His craft: his girl.

48

sweetness in his voice, the delicacy with which he gave mouth-to-mouth to the most unlikely material:

'"Kumbaya," man,' Robbie wailed. 'Freakin' "Kumbaya" and he did it straight and strong so Kamille and all her friends, they weren't minded to sickness. "Blowin' In The Wind", too. You remember how he'd de-mantle that for all our enjoyment? Kamille, she can't be doing with the grey-hair stuff but she was'—his writing swelled—'rooted to her sole place.'

It was perhaps inevitable that Robbie's letter would go on to end as it did. Perhaps he saw himself as a cross-cultural broker, a reshaper of imperatives. Perhaps—and I might have acted in just the same way—he saw a chance to steal the history of our schooldays and steer it to a different ending, an amendment to the constitution of our pocket-world back then.

I felt very alone when I finished the letter. Just me there, wherever that was. Then Thomas Hardy happened along. Headey's favourite poet, he was always on hand when our bête noire decided that what a lesson needed was a good old dose of Wessex cold and poverty. He seemed to get it right, too: did something to his voice when he recited yet another tale of carriage-cloth and missed chances, something that held fast to the characters of that ancient county in the long-away land that once twitched our country on one of its leading-strings. If I were to say that Headey in his recitative pomp would give the Voice of Grenada a run for his money…but I couldn't, ever. Still, whether our island rained or sweltered, he could conjure hoarfrost in Mellstock and drown our spirits in a hog-hole. Never more than with 'The Convergence of the Twain', whose meaning Esp once crisply summarised on an afternoon round Duttine's Cooler: '*Titanic* big, berg big, ship big-bigger, berg big-bigger—*I say, chappie, you're in my way, Chou poule brar! this my patch*—crunchin' and blammin' and t'ing and t'ing.'[21]

Thinking of re-convergence, I read again the end of Robbie's letter:

'…and they're an amazing band, a big pull, the nearest to proper Marley and Toots any hotel would allow. We'd love them to stay but they've been offered a cruise gig, four months, huge money. So I'm thinking, if Kamille's right, if he's got control of himself, if I can check him out before making the approach—who knows?'

Hardy and Mellstock and Otis and blammin' and Robbie and Kamille and *'This is meant to be a third-person narrative, Belmar'* and *'You want me to talk, Mr Headey? No, Mr Bond, I want you to siiing.'* Sometimes the voices come to me as if their only gifts are bafflement and loneliness. I guess I must have let them run crazy round my head then. I guess I must have gone walking out to the Minas Basin in almost properly summer weather. On the way I might have pictured Headey giving *La Galaxie Bleue* the once-over, then Esp peering like an abandoned child into the dark at the edge of those humming yard-gigs. I can't quite remember.

I remember next day, though. I was all set to answer Robbie's letter when the message came through.

---

[21] Blammin': slamming and banging.

7

God bless fluffy in-flight movies. They hold your attention just enough while giving it slack to feel good and warm about knowing how they'll turn out. Plus, there are certain situations where you just have to watch them. Say, if the alternative is a book or magazine you've already put down more times than you can count, and if you pick it up again you'll only go for a page or so before the headaches come curving back. Or a walk where you have no choices, unless you try to make it exciting by, say, counting the steps down the aisle from your seat and back or sliding for the toilet without being route-blocked by the stewardess's trolley.

Some guy lost his memory and ended up inheriting a fortune and a family of boys who'd never had baseball mitts surgically removed from their hands. How this came about involved a female lawyer, luckless with husbands, who'd given her nothing but grief and sons. Often she wept by the cliffs of Manhattan, only drying her eyes when she was flashbacked to her high-school prom in Des Moines where she rowed mightily with a geek (horn-rimmed glasses, problematic to keep on)—the guy, of course, destined to be the love of her life, but not for another seventy-odd minutes. Before that he kept bumping into her down the years in airports and hotel lobbies, now hunkily free of the horn-rims and squiring assemblages of curves and blonde hair that sometimes differed from each other by so much as the colour of a clutch-bag. She stared after him. He yelled Sayonara.

But everything changed when, pausing on a sidewalk to check his organizer, the guy was walloped on the head by a scaffolding bolt and the organizer slipped through a drain, followed by his entire life to date. After that he waded unseeing through a week of scrapes and comic interludes, his torment symbolised by shots of neon puddles inserted with finicky precision. One scrape involved a down-and-out whom the guy rescued from a bunch of desperadoes. The down-and-out vanished into the night but only after staring deep into the guy's face and stopping just short, I fancied, of telling him that the stare would mean something by-and-by. At last, with neither money nor bed for the night, the guy peered insensibly into a drugstore window. (The soundtrack music, hitherto feverish, stopped dead for that shot—a bold stroke, I thought.) Reflected behind him was the lawyer. He turned. She smiled and dabbed rain from his face. Nothing stirred in the guy's mind except the realisation that he knew her, had always known her, that she was the one and that was enough. He dabbed the rain from her face. She shivered. Well, it was cold and she'd only just got divorced again. This final, proper meeting, after all the blondes and departure lounges, was nowhere near Central Park—like the choked-off music, another innovation.

The down-and-out's meaningful stare came good, too. Before encountering the guy, he'd been living off the grid, sore at the world and its ways, but the desperado incident prompted him to make peace with his hearth, his slippers and the millions he'd made from his bespoke glove-puppet business, and as though sensing that the end of the movie was near, he'd resolved to do good and then tidy himself out of the way. Naturally he thought of his saviour. Through some improbable to-and-fro (was Thomas Hardy the patron saint of rom-coms?), the guy was summoned to the millionaire's deathbed and informed that he was his sole heir.

A year passed in a flash. The closing credits saw the guy leaning over the lawyer in a hospital room. In her arms was another son, theirs, one tiny hand restless, the other (no doubt mitted up already for the family team) hidden in a blue coverlet. I couldn't help hearing Esp's 'If You Don't Love Me' at the heart of the whole enterprise. By contrast, the other feature I saw—in which a pod of whales was in deep trouble off an English coast whose inhabitants all seemed to be weekenders called Rachel and Timothy—was almost briskly educational.

But those movies kept me in one piece after the message from home and during what was surely the most ornery route a squad of planes could have pieced together between Nova Scotia and Grenada. Toronto, Newark, Raleigh, Fort Lauderdale—at which point the schedulers ran out of ways to keep their birds safe in North America and one poor sucker just had to fly out across the water, stopping only at the Dominican Republic. Still, it was the best I could arrange, given the time-constraints, the amount of money I'd been wired, the well-meaning but leaky advice I'd had from Bob in the Main Street branch of Annapolis Travel.

But the flight wasn't all food for the reddening eye— weepy lawyers, a stunned paterfamilias saying 'Well, golly' at his ready-made family or the sun in the winter trees and, later on, whales consoled by elegant clauses.

As the relay of domestic planes handed me down the eastern seaboard and turned me over to the sea-leg, I found other ways to take my mind off the reason for my journey. Esp, of course, or The Voice of Grenada or Your Nowherian or whatever flag he was sailing under by now. Was Robbie about to check him out? Had he already, and was Esp, all things considered, now safe enough for *La Galaxie Bleue*? Pondering the ins and outs of that took me warmly back to the Harford days, right to the moment when I realised that Esp was willing Headey to splatter his work with ever more, ever redder condemnation. So short a time, so much history: I shuffled the memories during long stopovers, even in moments when the amnesiac legatee and the spike-heeled lawyer lost my interest. Once out of Lauderdale, however, and with the Barbour'd whale-watchers of the Kentish coast going only part of the way, I knew I had to work harder if I wanted to control my fear of what might await me.

Now I considered sticking-points for Esp's entrée into the world of lounge-music. First was, he'd tell Robbie to go fly a kite. That was no good: closed the whole thing down before it started. Replaying just that wouldn't last me between the final credits (the whales made out OK, by the way, save for one, trembly and aged, whose spout reminded me of a rebellious shoot of hair on Principal Tutela's head) and touchdown at Dom Rep-Punta Cana. So: first was, Esp said yes. Now—his stage-clothes. This was promising. Hotel bands had to be in uniform even when they weren't. It wasn't just a question of being chokingly brocaded or the boot-and-sombrero rules of mariachi. Smart-casual had its imperatives, too. If a reggae singer had wrinkles on his open-neck collar, his players had to get themselves wrinkled in kind. Being a solo act didn't let you slip this noose.

Esp's style was casual-derelict and many had been the school admonition heaped on him as a result. I imagined a chat, debate, war between him and Robbie in the matter, diplomacy mano a mano with zinging pride:

'What am I supposed to look like,' flamed Esp in my head, 'a Mousketeer? A Seven Dwarf?'

But at last a compromise was reached: an untorn golf-shirt, say, or a top with some kind of *Galaxie* logo which could be hidden the moment Esp swung his guitar into place.

But that still left the music: 'Freakin' "Kumbaya", man,' Robbie's letter had cried, aghast at this crater in Esp's new set-list, conveying the disbelief of informant Kamille. 'Blowin' in the Wind', too, had caught them on the hop. But she had to admit and Robbie had to honour her words: Esp had voodoo'd the songs, made them his own, seemingly freed the spirit of the first from its desolating repetitions, spread the elixir of youth over the second. But this was to do with something Esp had obviously spotted in them: recoverable worth, mitigating circumstance. Unearthing this, he'd chosen them, worked them in. Far different was having stinkers brought in from beyond the pale and imposed on him. I knew the ones and, sure as sure, so did he. Heaven knows, he'd destroyed them often enough for our delight. He'd bulldozed islands in the sun, wrecked banana boats, gone after 'La Bamba' like a madman with a new strain of Esperanto. And there were others, villains behind villains. The hotels lapped them up.

'The songs you're doing now are marvellous, Esp. I won't hear any argument against that.' In my mind, Robbie spoke with managerial ease, replicating the brightness that characterised his letters. 'But, as you are no doubt aware, our clientele...well, I'm not saying they don't want to be challenged, but...no, no, listen, listen, let me paint you a picture. They've been out all day...beach, water-skis...sampling'—maybe a nudge in the ribs here? No, forget it, perhaps not Robbie's style even now; make it a wink—'you know, Esp...sampling St George's treats. Happy times, Esp. Money laid down for our piece of paradise. Back they come in their cabs, on their hired three-wheelers. They're still excited but it's got to last, Esp. They've got to part it out for days yet. So the music, you see...the songs, the strains of nightfall'—where had I got that from? Probably one of Headey's shock-haired bards—'the songs have to be all about....' I stopped. Through the porthole window, day was starting to push at the blackness. Now: what would a manager-in-waiting say? What buzz-words would be gathered in his laundered arms? 'Tone. Tone, Esp. And balance. A bit of you...lot of you...with a bit of the *La Galaxie Bleue,* you see? Challenge and smoothness. Relaxation with a hidden edge. Now, your "Kumbaya"— amazing. Kamille...sorry, this is Kamille...she heard you one time in Grenville...and she was...Kamille, tell my good friend...see, Esp? Entranced. Which makes two of us...yes, I did check you out...exactly on her recommendation. "Kumbaya", eh? Never thought I could stand to hear that song again. So, if you think about it, it's just a small step from that to "Banana—"…no, listen, Esp, listen…'

The war that reignited kept me engrossed till we touched down at Port Salines.

8

My father was over the worst. I've no idea how it takes others but it almost literally burst out of him. While I was making my way through Robbie's last letters, a pallor was working deep into my father's skin, threatening him with beige. He dismissed it, but my mother didn't dismiss what she saw as evidence of a new level in his abstraction when he appeared among the family arrayed in bruises. Just there, he said: no, not carelessness at work, not a rumble or a spiteful doorway. But then, at supper one night, he'd leapt into the air, scratching his arms and chest as though tormented by whimsical booboo-men. In the end his belly had gone up like a balloon.

'A mean debility,' was my cousin Devon's assessment of the eruption. 'We thought he have the sugar[22] or his water all stripped out,[23] but this thing is deep ugly—a runaway train.' 'Runaway train', I found, was on everyone's lips. Perhaps it sounded more comforting than cirrhosis.

For a while there, things were confused. My homecoming was understandably lost amid tight lips, looks of distraction. I got to see my father on his penultimate night in St George's General. Most of the Harford family were there: the first time in nearly a year I'd been among the Brays en masse, and it took me a while to re-attune to the characteristic noise each made under stress. Sighs, whistles and prayers filled the

---

[22] Diabetes.

[23] Stripped of water—prostate illness.

scrubbed air. Only my mother just sat and stared at him, her look veering from Juliet to Medusa and back. Medicated, my father knew me and then didn't. His attempts to connect with his nearest and dearest were sabotaged by his seemingly involuntary curses at the General's laxity. Princess Alice, he slurred, was where he should have been taken. Hadn't he written as much…folded paper…in his check-shirt…or red one? This was news to everyone and my mother didn't seem to care about the spasm she induced when she said his red one had gone for washcloths a year ago. My sister Rosa, who for some time had been doggedly qualifying as mother's second-in-command in the matter of managing father—and who, I realised, had perfected a new, more distinctive sigh—cruelly suggested that he was in fact at Princess Alice. Hearing this, he inevitably pined for the haven of the General. My mother gave her a look which I hoped promised maternal anger but which seemed rather to suggest that Rosa was one step nearer her commission.

'I'll just'…just what? I had no idea. I wanted to be alone with my father and that wasn't about to happen.

'Go for a breather?' A hand lay on my shoulder: brother Tresford's, himself presently under the Headey yoke. Right beside me, quiet and consoling.

'Where's Marieve?' I directed the question at my mother but cousin Devon cut in:

'Back in Sauteurs.' Comfortable in the shadows she made bigger, rounder, my Aunt Lilly echoed her son.

'Way up'—my mother's eternal addition when speaking of the faraway place in which my next-oldest sister and her family had perversely chosen to live. Rosa made a cradling motion, giving the room to understand that our latest nephew, a frail battler, had again staked a prior claim.

'But she's coming down when Daddy's out,' Tresford assured me.

'And Dede's scooting right back from Kingston,' advised Devon, which triggered another of Rosa's new-minted sighs.

'Dede coming?' Father's voice could have been the last of water down a sink-hole.

'Mighty slow scoot,' muttered my mother. If Marieve's move to Sauteurs was hard to fathom, the life of mother's firstborn defied just about everything. Happily single, an administrating girl-Friday—no, girl-Crusoe—at the University of the West Indies at Kingston, Dede was father's favourite, loving and breezy, somehow contriving, when she came to visit, to be simultaneously within the family bosom and a yard or so outside it. I planned to learn a lot from her.

Tresford followed me into the corridor. We chatted for a short while, easy and unfussed: we could have been picking up a conversation from a day or so back. I commiserated about Headey. He said he'd show me his marked work—redder and splashier, he promised, than anything I'd brought home. Tresford crooked his thumb at the door:

'He go be OK. You know Ma. Got to be doing the Academy Awards thing.'

'It's Rosa that troubles me. She always wanted to be grown-up but when did she get so sour?'

'I keep telling her, knock it off. Doesn't suit her.'

'Ah, maybe she'll get tired of being Ma's shadow.'

'Yeah, well, the tiring can't come soon—'

'Tresford!'

I knew the routine from the bedsides of other ailing kin. The Brays took their hospital farewells in dignified stages. Tresford was required but, perhaps in deference to my journeying, or as emphasis that I wasn't in on the calamity from the start, I was this time exempt. With a shrug and a soft punch to my shoulder, he slid back round the door.

Turning, I saw a familiar figure approach, dart right and re-emerge moments later with two plastic cups. He motioned to an out-of-the-way bench, and we managed as firm an embrace as the coffees would allow.

'How fares my brother-in-law your father?'

I hesitated, at which Uncle Padmore nodded at the mournful door:

'Greek chorus making a meal in there?' His words filled me with warm memories. Among his many achievements was the ability to tell the plot-line of the *Odyssey* in ten minutes.

'Tresford reckons he'll be all right.'

'Tresford's head is on right-side firm-side. I was in there last night, adding my tears to the commonweal. Tonight I was detained. Breaking in our new whizz-kid.' He arched an eyebrow, started whistling something which he finally had to explain was *Deutschland Über Alles.*

'What's he doing back?'

'Bonn had a summer internship lined up for him but there were complications. So suddenly'—Uncle

61

thrummed the side of his cup—'back he comes, all set to count beans under Tony George's flag.[24] Well, our government needs him more than Germany's.'

'For permanent?'

'Uh-uhh.' He shook his head mid-swallow. 'He'll be back there in September—no doubt with my boss's oath of secrecy ringing in his ears. Can you imagine how we'd feel if Eric blabbed all our plans and our economy fell below Berlin's?' A passing sister shushed his volcanic laugh.

'Robbie Watts never said anything in his letters.'

'Ah, Mr Mitchell slipped under your boy's radar. Everyone's. Last-minute thing. But don't you fear—they won't let him slip away next year. He'll be a person of consequence round the Bundestag.'

I think I understood that, but he put me right anyway. Finishing his coffee, he went to find a bin and have a squint at the Greek chorus's progress. I turned my cup this way and that, realising that, machined though it was, this coffee was better than any I'd had up in the air. So: Eric and I had sudden homecomings in common. I wondered if the resemblance would end there. He had the prospect of departure at summer's end, a second year in Bonn and, from what Uncle had said and I'd long heard, a guaranteed future. But myself? Where had my turn of events stuck me? Already I was figuring what I might hear, perhaps that very night. Maybe not such a good scheme, Henderson, you taking off again, what

---

[24] Anthony C. George, designer of Grenada's post-independence flag.

with your father…We got one flyaway bird in the family, Henderson. Dede's enough. Money, Henderson. Maybe go see about cashing in your return. If your father hadn't fallen low, then OK, no call not to keep on with the books and snow and t'ing. But not now. Not OK. Lookit that Robbie Watts…if he can get a smooth step on the management ladder, surely you…. Money, Henderson. Maybe not such a good scheme. Dede's enough. Your father. Money.

I started. Uncle was peering down at me—having read everything on my mind? No surprise if so: he was an old-time diviner. And he'd certainly got something understood, suggesting as quick as he did that, after a last word or so with 'the ailing Chatterton', we should find a bar.

This was deemed a good move back at the bedside. Besides, everyone would soon have to leave, and father looked like he wanted to be left alone with his now-deflated belly. Uncle Padmore laid a priestly hand on his arm, avoiding the ghosts of two bruises, and said adios.

'See you soon, Dad.' Either my farewell was too scant or 'soon' sat balefully in his drug-woven mind, but he sat up in bed and pointed straight at me, necessitating much shushing and tutting and rescue of slipped sheets. Her glare indiscriminate, Mother got him settled again, but my presence now seemed to either terrify or anger him, possibly both. His mutterings came and went like a radio signal. What was I doing back? Were my studies to be thrown away? Who'd summoned me?

'You know damn fine who summoned him.' Mother spun at Uncle and me: 'Shoo,' she whispered, as though we were papaya thieves and she could see the stallholder coming.

Fifteen minutes later I was in half-darkness with life pushing all round, a beer on the table in front of me and Uncle saying, 'No, boy, no. You're the one.'

I'd tried to make my misgivings sound as serious as I could, to show that my year away had indeed begun to turn me into the thinker that Uncle's letters increasingly presumed. It felt, though, that my fear of not going back had come out in words better suited to the sniffles of a kid with a broken choo-choo train. Desperately, I'd just started on some hoary analogy—hitcher tries to get out of hometown, weeks pass, he's still rooted to the boundary line—when Uncle laid a hand on my shoulder, comforting my mouth shut.

'You're the one in this crew, Henderson. The walking man, the gleaner. Not just for the studying. You could stay here or go to Dede's place for that. Yes, your admirable sister struck out, but not a full strike, you see? She's not far far. Her arm is still crooked. Maybe she'll make it clean straight one day. She for certain could. But meantime and notwithstanding...you're the one who goes.'

I took solace from this—even from father's shook-up anxiety that I might have ditched Canada for good. Still, I wanted to be clear:

'But having to come back now. Unscheduled. I couldn't not but the cost was more than I could spare and the rest had to be wired through. That's extra from someone's pocket.'

Uncle smiled a moment and my suspicion about

whose pocket was confirmed. But he wasn't in the business of expecting salaams. As well as a diviner, he was a fixer, in the way that other people breathed and the Headeys of the world got mad. When he leaned forward, it was as if the matter of his sponsorship had never come up.

'Principal Tutela,' he said, 'all the folk who got behind the parish dollar-drives round St Andrew's. You think they want to see you kicking around back here? The whoever-it-was who signed off your scholarship up north. He might as well have practised his John Henry elsewhere.[25] OK, he can dish the remainder out to some other scholar-gypsy, no skin off his. But there's a bit of trust gone, you see? You signed up, too. Doesn't reflect well if you un-sign—for sure not on any Bray who says you should.'

'But what if Mother decides—?'

A finger, as portentous as father's from his bed but rather more controlled, shot out in the direction of the General:

'My brother-in-law your father will be fine. Believe your brother Tresford's word. What's happened is long overdue. I adverted to the state of play in my letters, and if all this hadn't erupted and you weren't called back to sit right here, I'd be adverting again, all along till it did. Your mother can be a ba-john with all you or she can be the Madonna, but she's never wavered in the matter of his weakness. Blind eye, blind eye, bit of cussing for form's sake, more blind eye, blind eye. Now'—he

---

[25] John Henry: signature.

65

steepled his fingers—'the boozing stops. And his weird side-kickery with that Headey'—his fingers flew open and he breathed across one palm—'dust.'

'It'll take some doing. Even for her.'

'She's seen the materiality of it. Him all raving and walrus'd in that bed. Does she want that? Would you? She'll get all Soviet on him henceforward. I know my sister when a thing has to be.' He chuckled. 'You can hear the bomb-doors open. And you'—he leaned closer still—'go back to your studies at the due and proper time. And you do not worry.'

The resemblance had never been more striking. Life had never allowed Mom to cultivate Uncle's easy style, but they were startlingly alike in delivering final words. A celebration of my relief was called for. When I came back with fresh beers, I found him disposed to reminiscence:

'I'd've stayed over there. God knows, not Roseville. Or even maybe England. But if I could have travelled on, that 'ssembly-line money in my pocket. Do other things when it got low. Seasonal. Pick stuff. Cast a line.' His eyes closed. 'The Algarve. Doesn't that sound beautiful? The Camargue. Places that got that long "a" to them—always enticing. It have pink flamingos in the Camargue. What do you reckon—Uncle P the flamingo farmer?' Laughing low, he cuffed my shoulder. 'But I wasn't a long-ranger. 'Sides which, life hasn't exactly run and hid from me here in the Spice Isle. 'Sides 'sides which, would've been just my luck to drop south from France and run slam into a Spanish Nettleton or something. The nettle-man. *El hombre de Ortiga*.' Again his laugh exploded as it had when the nurse shut him down. His cod-translation of nettle-

66

man brought back Eric's play all those moons ago. Milord and conquistador—and now, Roseville and Spain in their unlikely embrace. For a moment I was minded to reminisce myself, about that darkly eventful afternoon in Headey's class. But the urge went and I realised it was hardly an urge at all. Uncle's words had shifted things decisively. I saw Canada and my time there in a whole new light, just as I've seen my nowherian life ever since. I was the gleaner, the walking man—a matter of walking away from the old as much as towards the new. Sometimes more than.

Uncle could divine laterally, too. My memory-glimpse of that terrible afternoon put its key figure in play, as it were, above our table. It was an easy matter for Uncle to reach up, pluck down.

'So now you can relax and enjoy the gig.'

'Pardon me?'

'Mr Belmar. The Voice of All Us. *La Galaxie Bleue* tomorrow night. Second gig there—he must be doing right by the patrons.'

'Second gig? I didn't even know—'

'Man, I'd've thought your own informers would have prepped you.'

'Well there's been'—now I shook my hand in the direction of the General—'all this. A neighbour-lady said Robbie called by but we were at Aunt Lilly's.'

'Ah, our very own djblesse.[26] You see how she makes everything darker round my brother-in-law your father?

---

[26] A female devil.

She carries her own box of shadows, that one, 'case the day looks too healthy. Well, you can dodge her obeah tomorrow, and why shouldn't you?[27] You've honoured the invalid. 'Sides which, Eric's going, and I hear'—much nose-tapping—'Esp have Twinko alongside him. Quit his last band, Eric discovered. Probably'—again Uncle's stint in the Black Country came through and he became (as I later confirmed for myself) pure Ozzy Osbourne—'sum differunce of mewsikul duyrekshun.'

'Are you coming, Uncle? You've got it all found out. And you set him on the right road. Yes? Les Paul, Orbison? And then....' I clammed up, remembering too late his Nettleton letter, in which he'd castigated himself for the storm to which Esp's road had led. Clumsily I tried to face about, telling myself that Uncle's kindness to me deserved an assurance that what happened with Esp would have happened anyway, or something close. As well blame Les and Mary's tape-decks as himself.

But I'd lost him. He met my hashed attempt with a sombre pull at his beer:

'Best I don't re-hex the hex, Henderson.'

'Respectfully, Uncle, you couldn't have—' I was stumped by two moons right in my face: his eyes, fire-fierce. Again he was delivering a final word: not harsh but giving me to understand that his reasons were his reasons and would bear no fuss. Gambit over, he relented enough to console me:

'You report back on tomorrow. If he goes good, I might possibly swing by for the next.'

---

[27] Obeah: sorcery, witchcraft.

Once more particular figures were hovering in the air about us. Once more he plucked one down and named him:

'No card, no well-wish, not even the man's head round the hospital door,' he said. 'My brother-in-law your father could be deep under Carib Leap and Headey wouldn't care.'

9

Walking is a matter of away from as much as towards. More so. If I hadn't gone for that beer, if Uncle Padmore hadn't done his unmatchable thing, I might have been able to predict with some certainty how I felt about what happened later on. I might have felt again the spur of friendship, fury at indignities re-visited on one so little deserving of them. I might have perceived a thread linking my eager trawl of Robbie's letters for news of Esp to a sense of pride, of solidarity with the Voice of Grenada in a time and place that were fast approaching. Uncle Padmore had called me the gleaner, suggesting deliberation, an aim in view. Sometimes, though, gleanings just lie in ambush.

Tresford was right: things picked up. Next day my father was more obviously with us. He'd even tried, we discovered, to bear-hug a ministering nurse amid bleats of *My angel, my saviour.* But her nifty dance of escape left him tai-chi-ing the air before slewing over the bedside in a mess of water and pills. It was his gesture of thanks, he insisted to us, unbidden as the rains, at which my mother smoothed his nightshirt tight around him with the air of someone about to flourish the trussing-cords.

Marieve surprised us, turning up with her little girl and bearing love from all in Sauteurs, where her in-laws were in cooing charge of my fragile nephew.

'And how he?' asked my mother, allowing as always a truck-wide pause before that last word. RW was a no-good, her unshakable story ran. The one time he'd shifted his bamsee[28] was to abduct her second child to that distant, near-invisible star on which she was doubtless unhappy but, in chupid deference to RW and his crew, stayed wilfully dumb about it.

Affecting not to hear, Marieve bent deep over father and kissed his brow, whereupon little Candace, after a wide canter round the end of the bed, did exactly likewise from the other side. For a moment, mother's and daughter's hair meshed intimately, at which Rosa, who was doubtless hoarding a fresh stock of big sighs, just melted. I looked at her face, clearly at war with itself as she struggled to regain cred, to cuff away any mortifying hint that she could well be a mother of the future. But she was further embattled when word came through that, though she couldn't get away as hoped, Dede had called in some or other favour and arranged for father to convalesce at Montego Bay, details to follow. Fair play to Rosa: she made one last stand, her frame expanding as if to promise a sigh to rout the Red Queen. In an instant, though, she was pleading with my mother. She could be Daddy's chaperone (Daddy…so suddenly!)—couldn't she, couldn't she? Bon Jay, school was about done, she'd miss nothing.

'How you go do the national summer progression tests?' Judge-like, Tresford stared her down.

'What tests?' demanded Rosa and mother in unison. Candace twinkled: she knew Uncle Tresford to his bones. He knew that she knew, so he couldn't help his

_____

[28] Backside.

conspirator's wink. For my niece, the ensuing tumult was sweeter than candy.

I left them to it. I had to get weaving if I wanted to make show-time at *La Galaxie Bleue*. Father returned my Lone-Ranger salute, in which I tried to convey that all was well, that I'd be resuming my studies, as Uncle had it, in due and proper time. A tall order for a salute, tall as Esp's expectations of 'contraband'; and anyway, Marieve broke our contact, swaying helplessly, intoning 'summer progression' as biting-ant Rosa closed in on her. Squeezing Tresford's arm, I headed out, nearly colliding with the nurse who'd shushed Uncle the previous night and was now set on quelling the Brays. Mother was the last I heard before the dressing-down:

'Ask that Belmar if he et up that postcard you still waiting on.'

But the night didn't give me a chance.

10

La Galaxie Bleue was on the Grenville side of Harford Village on the Grenville-Upper Capital road. It was near what Eric had dubbed the St Andrew's Parish Strobe-Fest: in urban talk, traffic-lights. At the time, the island had one set of lights in Grenville and another in St George's. I don't know how many there are now. Last time I was home, there was querulous, hateful talk about the coming of speed cameras. But the lights were useful as a marker of a hotel's status. If you had strobes close by, that meant you were on acreage of consequence.

And *La Galaxie Bleue* looked the part. It was whiteboard-colonial, a two-storey affair of easy angles and verandah'd wings lazing out over the land. Here and there, a third storey was hinted at through little folly-like windows mid-way up the roof. White and colonial. Some imprints can't be tarred over. Then again, such designs go with heat and big skies. A slab of red-brick Gothic might attract initial interest but your average holidaymaker, especially a northerner, might not want to pay to park themselves in a replica of a commercial hotel in Manchester or Queens. Anyway, hotels are a bit like embassies: they become the official turf of whoever occupies them. Unlike diplomats, however, the patrons of Caribbean hotels aren't obliged to work round intractable oddities of local style. They require places that extend the feel and savour of beach, wave and palm. They part with good, perhaps even bad money for it. Boy, do they.

Even before I reached the front steps, the flow of languages and accents was sweeping down high and broad from the lobby. America predominated, although I was momentarily enchanted by tones of Oriental courtesy, and some English-brigadier voices, male and female, made me wince without thinking. The ground floor was as it always is: long, curving reception counter, battalions of phones, pigeonholes, public rooms called the Grenadine this and Half-Shell that, each with lush margins of foliage. Muted shrieks and splashes told of a pool somewhere beyond. At one end of the counter, a signpost with driftwood-y fingers indicated dining rooms, residents' bar, various walks and mezzanines. *Bar Mirabeau*, promised one finger, and I followed.

I found them at the bar, which was islanded in the centre of half-indoor, half-outdoor space. It was oval and straw-thatched, the latter a detail of the idealised Caribbean watering hole that international expectation has shaped into law. Radiating outward were tables and chairs. A waiter was just going the rounds to light a few discreet glass-cupped candles.

It was all arms around, a scrum without the bloodlust. Well, good night, here the jamoon.[29] You not ski here, Henderson? No, it's summer in Canada, too. So, how the gent? He's doing fine—last night in hospital. Po djab o,[30] that is some affliction. You tell him we wish him better than best. Hey, a long one? Robbie can get a tab rolling. OK, Robs? What you say, a tab rolling?—to France with that,[31] all I could do to get all-you in here without

---

[29] A star-apple: in my group, a term of affection.

[30] Poor devil.

[31] To hell with that.

commentary from above. You are every one with the band is how I framed it. Ah-sah, now Robs, Henderson have long-pull walk from St George's. Well, actually, I caught the—Hush, Canada…c'mon, Robbie, he's worth a drink, yeah? Eh-heh, since you say, he surely is and then some…ok, Henderson, what'll it be?

Robbie beamed at me as if affirming our bond of envelopes and postage. Honouring it, I insisted on getting the beers instead. He looked well. Something— the managerial life, maybe, or a sure sense of his home-bird place—had made him more than he'd been at school. His steadiness had deepened: no longer was he the peripheral man.

Greasing the wheels of talk, making the easy flow easier still, Twinko leaned in and out, rocking on the balls of his feet—sometimes so emphatically that he seemed like one of those toy figures you can never knock down. Beside him was his brother Ambrose, home from Caracas for a spell. I hadn't seen him in an age: we'd all been much younger when he took off. Smiling, reserved without awkwardness, he was obviously content to let his kid brother do the rocking and leaning. I imagined that, suspecting he might get little chance to use them, he'd handed Twinko a whole stock of words for the evening as happily as he'd let Eric have his guitar…

…which was sort of the topic we worked round to now. Twinko quizzed me on the Canadian music scene:

'Still all that grunge simmy-dimmy?'

'Not just that. They carry torches for Bob and Toots and the rest.' I drew a veil over the several fates that had befallen their songs at a campus folk-night Ian Paskin had dragged me to.

'That something. This one says it still have all them electro-jockeys where he is.' Twinko turned. 'What's that name mean, Kraftwerk?'

'Power station.' Eric was the same as ever, his voice momentarily stilling us with its unassuming authority. I wouldn't have been surprised to see telepathy at work, everyone at the tables producing pads and pens to await further translations.

'Always the way with buckras.'[32] Twinko drummed two fingers on the neck of his bottle. 'All they pop names must speak of chore and industry. Ain't the nine to the five what music's against?'

'Oh, Bonn's big on country 'n' western, too.' Eric smiled conspiracy at Ambrose as Twinko's theatrical revulsion doubled him up. I studied the smile. Eric was like our Dede on visits home: part and not part of the group, well into the cameraderie but equally happy, perhaps, if he suddenly found himself without. Now he'd clued us in on 'Kraftwerk', I figured I'd ask about 'swart'. From the afternoon of his play to now, I'd never heard or read it anywhere else. I could have looked it up but part of me was maybe holding off till a time like this.

But Twinko straightened up and demanded silence:

'Bottles charged.'

'Hey, hey....' Robbie was tamping the air down with his hands, evidently trying to head something off.

'Hey, hey, what hey, hey?' Eric leaned in beside Twinko. Ambrose nodded to the bartender, at which

---

[32] White people.

fresh drinks appeared in a line.

'Just the one per hand fuh now, compadres,' instructed Twinko, wagging a finger at Robbie when we'd obeyed. 'This man have just yesterday paid down on the manacles.'

'Why you such wajang, Twinko?'[33]

'And just listen how delirious it make him.' Twinko's bark of laughter lurched him backwards. Instinctively, Eric and I caught his shoulders and all our bottles rose upon the *Mirabeau* night.

But Robbie was flattered: his 'Nah…nah' came more in thanks than objection. Robbie the fiancé. The rest of us, I guess, moved up one.

'Sooo….' Twinko's arm was tight around him. 'We must seal the deal. A fete, Robert, big, en'less.[34] Port of Spain. Castries. Havanaaaaah.' Turning to us, he raised his bottle like a reporter's mike: 'The lady is, I may say, a cutie.'

I shook my head: 'You never wrote a hint of this.'

'When can we meet her?' asked Eric, pumping Robbie's hand. 'That is, can we?'

Robbie didn't answer. His name, growled like blasphemy, drew him away to where a little jug of a man was standing inside the bar entrance. The man embarked on much watch-tapping and pushed his face close into Robbie's. He pointed behind him and we could just make out a gaggle of people heading to where the evening's entertainment would be. This was some superior though

---

[33] Wajang: an uncouth person.
[34] Fete: a party, loud music, much to eat, dancing all night.

the term seemed wasted on a paunched and jowly type who was clearly up for intimidation. Robbie stood his ground, though, his occasional nods slow and reflective. He wasn't about to get into a step 'n' fetchit routine. Turning away, the man latched onto someone in the gaggle. We caught the sounds of glad-handing.

But the Robbie who returned wasn't the engaged beau who'd gone all aw-shucks at Twinko's teasing. His own watch was in plain view and his sigh was heavy above it:

'Yeah, he's just getting round to being late.'

Reabsorbed into a circle that had been broken for months, tickled by all the gas, happy as happy for Robbie, I only then remembered why we were there….

'He did this last night.' Robbie dug his hand in his pocket: suddenly the watch was not his friend.

'He never not done it any night,' said Twinko. 'Yesterday he lay traces and I knew just where to roust him out before the start. Today I've had no scent. Man, the way he go on…acting on latest t'ing in his head. Any wonder he took step south and ended in Caracas? Probably thought he was just off down the road.'

'And you saw him, yes? East Park?' Eric's eyes widened on Ambrose, who, having seen Esp last night, happily corroborated what Robbie's letter had relayed to me.

'That was him, confirmed,' he intoned in a deep, wide voice. 'Crazy right there. People were coming and going in the sunshine but he paid no mind. A dervish. Moko-boy.'[35]

---

[35] Moko: the devil.

'What did he do all those months? Rob said he'd been spotted a time or two, but—'

'Eric, he simply hasn't made himself available on the subject.' Twinko sank the last of his beer.

'Well,' said Robbie, 'I hope he makes himself available now. Look, I'd better go and prepare some damage limitation.'

'There'll be no damage. If he's no-show, me and 'Brose can do the needful. And this one here.' Twinko slapped Eric's arm and turned to me: 'He and 'Brose jamming earlier. He hot.'

Robbie sloped off…then, 'Ah-sah, I'd best support the guy. He out on a long limb for us'—and Twinko caught up with him.

Eric, Ambrose and I resumed our drinking.

'So,' I said, cradling my bottle, 'you're working with my Uncle Padmore.'

'He's only just been breaking me in. I was planning a summer in Bonn but there were compli—'

Complications: yes, Uncle Padmore had said as much and it was just as well because Eric's half-word was all the answer I got. Now his gaze drifted off a way, and his face looked just as it had when Esp was explaining his dizzy hopes for the meaning of 'contraband'. Ambrose and I peered hard at him. Perhaps my Uncle had put a bit of divination my way. I followed Eric's gaze, guessing what I'd see.

He came threading through the far tables, his guitar riding his body like a bandolier. When he saw us, his hand convulsed like a tic-tac man's: salute, lordly sweep, peace-sign. But he didn't come near: maybe he was just deep in Esp-world, running on Esp-time…or something had told him that the crowd would soon be *in situ* and Robbie was beginning to…or the little jug-man was already very seriously…. Whatever, we could have been just a bunch of guys at the bar.

Robbie intercepted him at the bar entrance but his emphatic 'Phew' was wasted on the Voice of Grenada, who just nodded and shouldered his way round the corner. Like Hamelin's children, the rest of us followed. The chat in the bar faded behind us as, from another direction, the burble of nations rose, multi-toned, restive. A portion of their hard-earned money was supposed to be looping back to them in the shape of tonight's melodies. OK…so when? asked their anticipation. Soon enough, now that Esp-time had bumped into the world's. Inwardly echoing Robbie's 'phew', I pushed through the lobby…and faltered. A gap in the crowd revealed a figure wearing what Uncle would call Aunt Lilly's best shadows. Familiar? A trick of the light and noise? There was no time to investigate. Robbie called us on:

'Got you seats. Since you're with the band,' he added with emphasis. Perhaps the little jug-man was in earshot. He seemed the kind who was never out of it.

11

Alhambra was a funny, mish-mash choice: I thought, anyway. There was that guitar piece, 'Memories of the Alhambra', which Uncle Padmore had and hadn't taught himself, half-humming, half-whistling the melody while he strummed the chords. He served up the next connotation, too, all those Midlands movie-theatres in which he'd heard 'Infamy! Infamy! They've all got it in for me' and 'This here's Miss Bonnie Parker. I'm Clyde Barrow. We rob banks.' The Regal. The Essoldo. The Alhambra ('Wellington Road, Bilston, boy, and still going strong when I left. All Asian stuff, hours long, princes and slave-girls and "hey, let's sing this here argument instead!" I got pally with some Bengalis, we used to go. Solidarity, I guess. Those movies were colourful like colour was long gone from fashion, but you would not sit down to them unfed'). Then of course there were the Moors and ancient Spain: we knew about them, in and outside school, rather younger Spain having left its mark round and about our sea.

Perhaps the management had decided that Alhambra-ness was a point of convergence for its likely patrons, a cultural touchstone they'd all recognise, like Vivaldi in an elevator. And, fair's fair, the *Alhambra Lounge* wore its pretend history with gusto. The windows were arched in bright, sandy wood, fretworked at the top. Pillars which may or may not have been load-bearing marched down the sides of the room. Set into the walls, flame-shaped electric torches writhed and darted convincingly. Only in one corner did Moorish tradition yield: bottles, optics, labels with grouse and paddle steamers and monocled dandies. And the jug-man, beadiness itself as he gazed about. Fascinating, it was, the feel of the room, made even more pick 'n' mix by the jumble of skin-colours, accents, clothing at the tables around me. This was their brief home but it called up the obsolete and the contradictory to furnish their comfort. Moors necking beers? No, not then, not now. Perhaps, in line with some principle not easily explained, hotels were places to make travellers feel harboured and unsettled at the same time. I was minded to ask Robbie.

Before us, a slightly-raised stage was edged, like the other ground-floor rooms, with foliage. It was hard to tell whether it was well-nurtured or artificial. If the former, its hues and shine suggested plate-glass roofs with endless sun above. Before one toy palm, Twinko was checking the skin tensions of a conga and a djembe. Two mikes were in place but there was no other hint of a sound system; perhaps it was concealed in the greenery along with a mixer. Upstage centre, just outside French windows with an arch of particular extravagance, the Voice of Grenada or Our Nowherian seemed to be pacing. At any rate, he reared up a moment, disappeared, reared again, the body of his guitar briefly flashing this way and that.

Our group weren't alone in tracking this enigmatic semi-absence.

'Has he an anxiousness?'—the voice, a table or two along, was maybe Swedish. Instantly placeable was a rejoinder from nearby:

'I coulda stayed in St George's 'stead of this. Heard he was good last night but if he's just gonna…hey, buddy, you lost your guitar instructions out there? I can call my son in Denver, get him to send his.' The man's raised voice prompted a slow, raggedy handclap from the tables round about.

'Manman o'[36] came from the back of the room: the jug-man, I guessed, his splintery tone as unappealing as the rest of him. 'Watts, you get him and start in now fuh now.'

Twinko gave Robbie a *no sweat* look and strode to the grand archway. Robbie took the stage.

'Ladies and gentlemen, now fuh now—our way to say this instant, without further ado—he hit the heights last night and he'll do it higher and better tonight—with Twinko the premier skins-man of the Isle of Spice—we give you your own wanderer, troubadour, mystic Nowherian—the Voice of Grenada!'

'That's smooth all right,' whispered Eric. 'Better than Edward Heath when he let us go. Think we'll be voting for Watts down the road?'

I thought nothing. Twinko barely had time to get back to his drums before Esp came circling downstage, jostling fronds and rocking a pot or two. At least one of my in-flight fears was allayed: however tortuous his negotiations might have been, they had ended with him passingly clad in a sports shirt and jeans that more or less kept to two shades of rust.

'Well, praise God and pass the bourbon,' said the voice that had enquired after Esp's guitar instructions, and the applause rose, tricked out with whistles and, here

---

[36] Oh, mother!

and there, admiring female yelps.

Esp raked us all with staring eyes. Legs apart, guitar swung into place, he looked, for all his moody defiance, as though he wanted to dart out again or at least hunch up. He did not look well. Nor did his salutation—'Good evening, my *Galaxie Bleue* crew,' delivered like a misfiring Johnny Cash—do anything to restore confidence. How different Twinko looked, smiling easy, rolling one and the other shoulder in preparatory work-out, set to tumble about the drums with his by now much-admired 'anyone can do this' genius. He flicked eyes left, caught a nod from the Voice of Grenada, and we were off.

'Slip-Slidin' Away?' A Buckra song to kick off? But Paul Simon's lament on the impossibility of finding life's destination worked a treat to ease the crowd in. Its melody was as happy as the lyrics weren't. Besides, it was no doubt one of the casual popular anthems in the daily life of the barracker and his pals seated along from us. Esp even went a tad calypsonian in the chorus. A neat choice…

Next came a couple of his own recent songs, introduced with a quiet levity which divorced him from the ranter Headey had bundled from the classroom. Full of light and space, allowing Twinko to do some tasty slaps on the rim of the conga, they sustained the Simon feel, even if some of the rhymes—'unserviced cars / like 'splosions on Mars' at one point—forced on Eric and me a mutual 'ouch' of which we were instantly ashamed. They were good, though, ease-plus-oomph, permitting me to think for a moment that, whatever Esp had been through in the missing months, some part of his music

84

had emerged nicely seasoned.

'Many Rivers To Cross' was and wasn't a shock. So: at some point he certainly had ditched his attitude to our islands' big names. On the other hand, he'd made the song his own, Jimmy Cliff's pleas giving way to calmness, at times almost a whisper. Maybe this was Esp's autobiography, the nearest we'd ever get to hearing about his strange absence. For sure he rose up out of quietude on the chorus, giving it nails. Whether in fact or in his head, he'd taken on river after river.

The crowd were loving it. Nearby, the Swedish-sounding voice dipped in and out of any familiar bits, while the chorus of 'Many Rivers' caused the American posse to roar and clink glasses. Just behind me, a group of Japanese sighed loud at certain of Esp's inflections as though, at the last second, he'd brought off a daring haiku. Swaying over his drums, Twinko had the dreamy, hopeful look of someone who thinks they might just get through and enjoy themselves on the way. As for Esp, his stance grew more natural, more like he wanted to own it. Now and then he'd nod appreciatively at the crowd as though he was already working through a bunch of encores. I should have noted that nod…

…but, with the crowd warmed up, we were back in 'Ponents land. A run of old favourites brought Esp's phantom buddies stealing from the wings. Elvis whispered his moves, the Big O swelled his voice; Otis was on hand to buff the footwork. Sex and grace: more yelps from the women. We were well into 'If You Don't Love Me' before I knew it and he took the song at such a lick that 'contraband' fitted as never before.

'*Now* it sounds like it should,' whispered Eric as Elvis and the whole crew fired up Esp's body for the once, twice, thrice of the final chorus. I thought of my plane journey, of one of the exchanges I'd given Esp and Robbie as the hours and clouds flowed by. Tone, I'd made Robbie say. I need tone and balance. You and *La Galaxie Bleue,* Esp, the raw and the smooth. Gee the crowd up but, so help me, don't get them in a skitter. Whether or not any such words had passed between them, Esp was taking the challenge on his own terms. Another river for him, this gig, richly wide and deep but full of ornery currents, needing a certain kind of tickle to make it flow one way. His initial awkwardness had made me wonder if he were cowed by what were obviously the most formal surroundings he'd ever sung in. But there was none of that now. He was winning. He was giving them all kinds of edge and they were taking it without a twitch.

The applause was even more boisterous. Under it, the Japanese group behind me renewed their oohs and ahs, which Eric caught too, whispering 'Someone wants to take him home.' Even as he spoke, I caught sight of a note being surfed to the front. It reached Twinko but a sculpted, braceleted hand gestured its re-direction to Esp. Reading it, Twinko clapped a dramatic hand to his brow, prompting a burst of giggles, before handing it on.

'Esp don't want to waz away all his strength up there. He need five-lady reserve.' Ambrose's words reached Robbie, sitting tight against the stage, and his laughter met our own. Now Twinko was tilting his head, letting his lip protrude like a lorn pierrot. Sure enough, another

86

note came his way, the sender pointing to herself, tossing her blonde hair. As for Esp, he nodded again, first into the crowd—presumably at the lady or ladies who'd claimed him for after-hours—then straight at Eric and me. I assumed he was connecting properly with us at last, making up for his absorbed shuffle through the *Bar Mirabeau.* In sharper circumstances, I might have thought otherwise. The only comfort now is that it went over Eric's head, too.

Well, then: 'Blowin' in the Wind'—raved over by Robbie's co-worker Kamille, testimony to the skill (genius?) with which Esp could kidnap a song and erase its history. Whether Twinko knew it was coming up wasn't clear. He waited for Esp to strum a while, then, with the slightest frown and lip-twitch, slid a bossa-nova beat underneath which met with the Voice of Grenada's approval. We settled back to enjoy. From around us came sighs and handclaps of recognition. The song belonged to the world and who knew what differing images it conjured in the minds of the listeners? Earnest European protest, America at one of its many crossroads, memories of hearing or using it as a lullaby, of playing it over and over on record players of German, Japanese, British make. My uninformed guess was that the Americans beside us willingly surrendered their everyday image of Dylan as a godfather of whiny freaks and bathed in the knowledge that, like hula-hoops and the Mouseketeers, he was something they'd dispatched round the globe.

Tenderly came the first verse, the first-time chorus. Orbison and Belafonte could have been standing right behind Esp, having shaken hands on co-sponsoring the vibe. But the second verse was different. The sponsors might have turned awkward then, looked away, shuffled their feet. Dylan's sneer infected Esp, lasting into the third verse and chorus, but then Esp dismissed him as a moody amateur and hit for himself. Something else took hold of the song, a dark presence among the foliage. This was no longer a troubadour's plea for us to think and hope: it was a misanthrope's fart. Twinko looked across at Esp, then down at us, puzzled, fearful. Fangs bared, Esp churned through the verses. Again and again the chorus came, bleaker, bleaker, crying as if under torture that as well as no answer there was no wind, no world, no point to such a half-assed song. For the last repeat, Orbison and Belafonte were summoned again, the renewed tenderness so misplaced as to be obscene, like in a filthed-up carol. He'd erased the song's history, all right, and whatever compassion it held.

'Thank you, thank you,' crowed Esp without waiting for any response. Hunched down, Robbie crept back to us from the stage:

'That's not how Kamille said—' he began to me but others cut him off:

'What's eating you, buddy? Sing 'em straight.'

'Sir, are you vexed? Should we ask them to lessen the lights?'

'"Shrimp Boats," Esp, darling,' said a voice out of Buckingham Palace fifty years ago. 'Never mind the silly protest stuff.'

'Pardon me, lady, I think you'd better—'

But with a pantomime cackle, Esp confounded them

all, Twinko included, by launching into Bobby Darin's 'Beyond the Sea', during which he dragged in and mangled the original French, possibly to endear himself further to his lady friends. Still hunched, Robbie moved circuitously back to the stage. I watched his progress, so slow that he seemed to take just one step for each line of the song. Back at his post, he smiled up at Twinko and then at the patrons nearest to him; nodded his head, affecting to get into the song that Esp was now treating so gently. He was rattled. Inside, I guessed, he was all knots. Twinko found a groove he could enjoy about a verse before the end. Amid the relieved applause, the cries of 'That's it, pal, that's what we pay for,' he swung at Esp with arms folded. Esp just grinned back.

'Chou poule,' murmured Ambrose, understandably concerned for his brother. 'Esp best leave that blowin' wind alone. His grip loose.' More to the point was Eric's 'shuhh.' Hasty whispers confirmed us in one mind. For some reason, Esp was messing at the edge of sabotage. Good money, female favours and still he was set on manufacturing an ulcer apiece for Twinko and Robbie. For some reason…? Pretending to stretch, I stood up and looked about. No sign of the familiar figure I might or might not have spotted in the lobby. But we were packed pretty tight here in the *Alhambra* and everyone looked like an Impressionist daub. Esp barracked me back into my seat without mention of my name or any close connection. Again I was some guy at the *Mirabeau* bar as he came loafing through. I sat down but inside I stayed standing—ready, I see now, to start the walk away.

The first-half closer was another of his songs: a sub-

Donovan thing, pretty decent—decent enough to suffer an image of a couple gazing from a beach at a cloud with dreams to teach. New song or not, it did its business. A lazy shuffle, generous, fat chords. You almost expected to feel the surf on your shirt. The audience was back in Esp's palm. Twinko was clearly loving it—or loving the fact that, in a verse or two, he could have sulphuric words with Our Nowherian. Esp looked more chilled than any time in the set—that business with Dylan and the post-nuclear wind might never have happened—until, as the song neared its end, that staring yard-gig look came back into his eyes and he took a pace or two left and right. Now Eric was onto it. Twisting round, he half-rose but courteous Japanese dismay turned him back.

'He's not looking out for—? Oh, man,' he whispered as the song ended, Robbie sprang up with, 'Beer break, folks—twenty minutes,' Twinko called 'Thank you, 'preciate it' and, cloaked in yelps and clapping, the Voice of Grenada wheeled round and stalked off through the French windows.

The main lights came up and Eric, Ambrose and I stood aside to let those around us head for the un-Moorish bar. 'Singer got a tad goofy back there,' said one of the Americans as he shoved by. Robbie was about to join us when some hectic clapping deflected him towards the bar, where the jug-man was looking daggers his way. 'Come on,' said Eric, and we scurried over the stage past the overdone foliage.

Out back, Twinko had Esp trapped in the angle of two fences and was having a mighty say:

'…so you best not screw like that second-half. This is

90

a good thing, fine money, hot craft all fuh laying themselves out and that, *that,* is my one sole 'centive for doing horse-shit Dylan and "Kumbaya" and where'd that "Beyond the Sea" come from, did we go through it? no we did not, so next time you're minded fuh *voyer, voyer,* make it known, shit, write me a letter and p'raps I'll find some beats I can live with for the whole duration. Now brar, this is straight and this is in the cross-hairs, 'f you wan' do Prince of Darkness t'ing you go shake up all the workaday bamsee in St George's. Hell, Headey walks there, I seen him, which I sure ain't here at the Blue Gal.'

Eric and I exchanged glances. 'Headey?' mouthed Ambrose, at which Eric leaned to his ear:

'Long story—longer than we'd hoped.'

Esp met Twinko's assault with a look that might have suggested deep serenity or someone about to nod off. Twinko grabbed his shoulders for a final push:

'Listen to me, Nowherian, get over Headey, get over yourself. After all this time? Headey just landfill, man. He here? He not here? Ten of him here, make no twitch difference. Pay, tips, béké bamsee—we do better two night than he do month.[37] Two night come more night, fine fuh me, I play 'God Save The Queen' with my chin to keep all that going. You won, man. You been who knows where you been but Headey still stuck in him shack of a world. Quit your big stares, quit the arseness.'

Robbie found us then and, with a blood-stopping hug, Twinko brought him in:

'This man here, this man on brink of love

---

[37] Béké bamsee: white (female) derriere.

'sponsibility, this man out on long limb f'us, it does have deep grief already fuh this man from his squitty boss. Look on this man—you want his ruination?' Twisting a little in the drummer's grip, Robbie tried a sort of *yeah, you look here* meanness. But he just wasn't mean and the look went all hammy and glazed. Eric and I shifted forward as though this would supply Robbie's lack of edge. Ambrose just looked blank.

At last, Esp gazed round at us one by one, his expression all jolly-old-pals. We could have been back in school, buoying him up that time Flutter Priestman turned him down for the concert. He opened his mouth and for a second I had an urge to plant one on it. Foolish, no doubt, to expect any contrition—but was it too much to ask that, given the smorgasbord of pay, tips and bamsee laid out by Twinko, he'd at least call a truce with his own demons? What came out instead was an old man's chuckle, phlegmy, weird—smug, somehow, as though he were pondering stuff for him to know and us to find out. Whether or not he twigged this, Ambrose jerked forward:

'My brother being awful tolerant, Esp—all we same so. It have no further need for any cunumoonu nonsense.'[38] He didn't raise his voice but the look in Twinko's eyes implied that physicality wasn't unknown to his diffident brother. It might have been better if Twinko had kept hold of Esp. Suddenly he was gone, back-vaulting over the fence. Like an out-of-it Cheshire Cat, all he left us was more of that phlegmy chuckle.

---

[38] Cunumoonu: a foolish person.

Now Ambrose worked fist in palm and Twinko released Robbie in order to calm his brother. Rubbing his arm, Robbie worsened the mood: it seemed that one of the Americans had pinned the jug-man against the wall and imposed a bet that Esp wouldn't finish the second half.

'What, and he took it?'

Robbie stared at Eric. Never had a love-'sponsible beau looked more dismal:

'Probably staked my wages.'

A claxon shattered the night. Twinko looked about wildly:

'What is this, *raid on, duck and cover*?'

'Second half.' Robbie cuffed his arm. 'I'll get fresh drinks up for you and…hey, thanks.' As he sloped off, Twinko called, 'Lookit, Robbie—the brainpower here. Bray and Mitchell. You need a testimonial, they do it sweeter than the first turd of the day.'

Emboldened, perhaps, by this singular guarantee, Robbie's shoulders straightened as he went in through the windows.

Voices were swelling behind us. Ambrose, Eric and I decided that it was politic to skirt round back and come in through the *Alhambra* entrance again. The first thing I saw was a figure dipping and rising among the tables. I thought it was a fussy punter making a big to-do of finding his seat. But it was Esp, laughing, shaking hands, patting shoulders, working the crowd. Already onstage, Twinko stared blankly at him from the rampart of his drums—hoping, perhaps, that this glad-handing signalled good behaviour from here on out but not trusting a single move of the Nowherian's wiry body. But then the blonde who had surfed a note to him came up and, giggling, clattered his djembe and began a mess of hair-fiddling. I smiled—and was envious. Perhaps, whatever happened, Twinko could lose himself in bliss after all.

'You behave yourself, Esp,' called Eric as we passed near. 'And up there.'

Turning round, Esp made one of those gestures that spangly types use on TV spectaculars as, sprinting down a staircase, they catch someone's eye. Here was the pointing finger, here the *hey, great you could make it* twinkle…which, of course, masks *who the hell are you?* Moments before we'd been gathered round him out back, his oldest friends, concerned to back Twinko and Robbie but also to block his own mad leap off the rails. I wondered what I was doing there. It must have been then, I guess, that my inside Bray started his walk.

The lights dimmed again. Balladry began the second half and the crowd, hand-pumped and chin-chucked by the star in the interval, fell right in with it. 'Cupid,' 'Only the Lonely'—Sam and Roy trading the greatest of their hits, and it was beautiful, Twinko's beats snaking over and under Esp's pretty guitar, Esp's voice pure, free of the torment of whatever rivers he'd crossed in his missing months. Now the ladies who'd chosen them were laughing and 'yes, yes-ing,' and the head American near us called out 'Lucky sonsabitches', to the mirth of several. After that Esp sang 'Blowin' in the Wind' again, sweet as a nut. From his dugout by the stage, Robbie looked all forgiveness at him. This, I assumed, was the way Kamille had heard him do it, giving it new but not

94

feral life, pressing the buttons without stabbing them loose. I remembered how Robbie had quoted her. If she were here, she'd be rooted to her sole place all over again. When he was done, Esp gave a minstrel's bow to the audience, receiving 'Now that's a sight better' from the head American. You'd have thought that Esp was about to go into that flummery you get at the end of some Shakespeare plays, when a confection of plumes and weskit heads to the front of the stage and says, well, we're not much but hope you didn't nod off, mind how you go.

And Esp sauntered over to where his drink was and took his time swigging it, and Twinko—more relaxed than I'd seen him all evening—opted to do the same, and there were whoops from here and there, and the Buckingham Palace voice said to a friend, which is to say the room, that it was all very jolly, and one of the Japanese people called out, 'You extremely good' to the animated embarrassment of his party, and this brought fresh applause and 'You tell 'em, stranger' from the American camp, and Esp set down his drink and glided back to the centre of the stage, and Twinko rubbed his hands with a confidence that said he was ready for a fine song, and Esp opened his mouth and Robbie gave him the thumbs-up. After that, Esp sang *Woo—woo—woo— woo* twice, acapella, and we feared what was coming and he tucked in the chord changes and we knew and Twinko froze.

Well, they all knew the song. They leapt on it more merrily than on 'Blowin' in the Wind,' this cheesy speculation about making big noise morning and evening all over this land in the service of justice, warning, love between this and that one. It was the kind of song you felt you'd heard even if you'd never heard it—though a glance at Twinko's face showed that it was also another kind of song, compared to which 'Beyond the Sea' was up there with Marley. But he recovered and got in under it with a suitably chunky beat and thereafter fixed his face at some point between indifference and Chou poule!

Ambrose gazed at us, at Esp, at his brother, back at Esp. He said nothing directly but, under the gathering flow of the song, I heard him wonder whether Esp had really heard what Twinko was saying out back in the interval. Eric, too, was speculative:

'Isn't this drivel what you'd close the set with?'

Yes, it was—or what you'd throw in as an encore when no one knew or cared any more. I looked across at Robbie, the jug-man now squatted down behind him. He was happy as Larry—looked as he probably had when his girl said 'yes': ready to cry 'hello, birds, hello trees', scarce able to believe the world's benison.

Even after all this time I can't listen to that song, certainly not the opening gush, all the *Woo—woos*. Esp gave the crowd a generous shot of those, seven or eight, to get them all in the required zone. When it came, the first verse was like 'Many Rivers to Cross', his voice and guitar dipping, going prayerful. When he wished he had a hammer, he sounded almost contrite, like he'd have no time for such objects in the usual way of things, but…well, you know, you can't let justice and love hawk themselves about these days, ain't that kind of a world, you just have to be their booster. Robbie tried to catch

96

Twinko's eye but Twinko resisted. Perhaps he didn't want to let slip his own apprehension, infect the moony bliss of the manager-in-waiting. Instead he snuck a sideways look at the Voice of Grenada, his eyes saying everything and nothing. Then we were back in the *Woo—woos,* maybe six this time, getting the audience's backs bolt-straight, getting their hands clappily over their heads, musical Calpol.

Then came the wish for a bell—louder. Well, alright, bell-chimes weren't small and thin, they meant celebration, decree—unclean, unclean, too, but let that go. Esp doubled the rhythm, taking it to the edge of a flamenco-y thrash. I saw him as Ambrose had, going bananas in Caracas's East Park. Twinko had to up his volume and this split the audience, the Americans, the groupies and the Buck House functionary all romping along with it but some others half-shaking their heads, letting their hands fall after losing clap-time. Esp saw, let the schism widen just so much, then sweetly whooshed them all into another bunch of *Woo-woos*: seven this go round.

Heaven knows which of Esp's sponsors took on the verse about wanting a song to sing. Engelbert Humperdinck was in contention: Esp's jaw was set in just his way, as it had been when Headey shut down his bravura that afternoon. But someone else was in there, snatching at the mike. Elvis, Roy, Sam, Otis, they were all on a break. Never Pavarotti? Yes, for a warble or two. And wasn't this the Great Caruso himself, breaking justice, warning, love into swoopy syllables? The Japanese party loved it—maybe they thought it was karaoke without any miscued backing. Robbie was still on cloud nine. Behind him, the jug-man was nodding his head up and down, left to right, doubtless secure in his loony bet: Esp, it seemed, was staying put for the paid duration. As for Twinko, he'd decided to gift all of his efforts to his new lady-friend, swaying away at the front, occasionally plastering Robbie's face with her silken hair. *See, this singer,* his expression seemed to say, *I only met him tonight.* Ambrose seemed happy for his brother, though there was still something not quite settled about him. Eric was leaning forward, hand on chin.

The thing about monochrome foliage is that anything against it stands out clear as day.

'Jesus H!'

'Esp, honey, no!'

'Sir, is this a wise spectacle?'

The guitar was flat on the stage. Sheer professionalism kept Twinko on the beat, but only his fingers moved. Dragging Robbie to his feet, the jug-man waggled his arms about: 'What this?'

'I'd hammer out warning,' whispered Eric as he, Ambrose and I rose up.

Under the low lights, against the greenery, the knife glittered and spun. The quicker it moved, the fainter Esp seemed to grow until he could have been one of those black-cloak puppeteers. The knife floated along the lip of the stage towards and away from Twinko, towards and away. It stabbed out, randomly menacing space above saucer-eyes, other figures rising. Like a puppet, it sang words not its own, half melody, half breathy hiss, as of someone running through a number before curtain up:

98

'*Fi had a knife…slaughter in the morning…in the evening…all over this land…slaughter your justice…freedom…ev'ry prick that calls me brother anna sister…*'

'Buddy,' cried the head American, the 'Jesus H!' man, 'we forgave you the Dylan and got back on your side. This…you know what we do to guys—'

The knife was now back among the foliage, the tip of the blade darting like a robin. The voice escalated:

'*What we do to guys…'slave 'em in the morning—*'

'Hey…hey, hey, hey, you hush, that's long gone.'

'*Never ever gone,*' countered the breathiness, '*never ever long gone.*'

Pushing to the stage, Eric, Ambrose and I were buffeted by tans and cleavage falling back. Head down, arms out, the jug-man pushed Robbie into our path as if he were freight on a ramp, then retreated himself, maybe deciding that only by swelling our posse of intervention might his underling hope to keep his job—or that, whatever we did, his bet still had life if we kept Esp onstage. To our right, the head American and a couple of pals were likewise closing in.

Seeing the massed approach, the knife-tip shivered among the foliage, wagged up and down like an old man laughing at the chupid pride of those who would teach him a lesson. I expected to hear that wheezy chuckle, the only answer Esp deigned to give us out back during the interval, see phlegm snake along the blade.

He'd tried. All this time Twinko had tried. He'd drummed a counter-footfall as we moved to the front. Anyone with an ear for that kind of thing might have said that the savagely eager Americans had got up expressly to embroider his beat. Professionalism again: hold it together, show goes on. Besides, Twinko had seen us all coming. If I'd been him, I'd have thought, yeah, let them deal with it, I've been booked for this. But really there was no show now, nothing to hold—and with a sweeping look of anger that took all of *Alhambra* in and forced a cry—fear? excitement?—from his lady, Twinko bowled his conga aside and crossed the stage before us to where the bird-knife was now deep among the leaves. The knife shot out past his shoulder and Esp sprang into view before the French windows, trapped our gaze with his hand and reached into his sportsshirt.

'If I had a gun,' cried the emerging hand and we all hit the deck.

No coming back from that...the windows swung open and, in the pin-drop silence, Esp's footsteps ended with a thud on softer ground. Finally someone turned up the lights.

'Asshole!' came the jug-man's weepy boom.

'C'mon...c'mon, c'mon, c'mon.' A warm voice. A brotherly voice.

So up I went and was presented with what looked like a chair-strut cut in half. I listened, tapped the halves, fell in as best I could. Sometimes there a whistle whenever I sounded, or at least looked, as though I'd got it right.

It took about a minute. Hand on heart about that. No more than a minute after Esp's disappearance. I've never seen anyone move so fast. He could have overtaken Esp if he'd been so minded and still had enough puff to flay him alive. Instead, understandably, Ambrose's thoughts were for his brother. No more than a minute. In the time it took to register that Esp was no longer even a footstep, Ambrose leaned and whispered to Eric—who vanished through the main entrance—took the stage, clapped Twinko on the shoulder, swung the abandoned guitar to his ear, checked the tuning, got his brother back to his drums with a *follow-me* nod, started in on a soft flow of chords, waited till Twinko was comfy enough underneath them and gave a grin as wide as all get-out to the knots of punters about to exit, to the head American and his pals still glowering—perhaps at their own thwarted anger—by the front of the stage, to Robbie, to the distraught jug-man:

'What knife?' demanded his grin. 'Whatever gun?'

…and what diffident Ambrose? Smooth, smooth— God, that grin could talk. Hesitantly they returned, edged to their old seats, to the drinks and stuff abandoned on the tables. Now Ambrose's grin was saying how that scampering mad-ass would be dealt with, late or soon. Even so, some stared hard at the French windows, the foliage. Yes, they'd seen him go or, while hunkered down in fear, heard neighbouring relief that said so. All the same…but Robbie skirted the new line-up onstage, closed the windows and skirted back. He looked enquiringly at the jug-man, nodded backwards, mimed the turn of a key. The jug-man gave a mean little shrug. The mad-ass had scampered off with his bet. OK, everybody still there, happy again, would drink more, no blood on the carpet. Still, what did he care about keys and windows? Ducking into shadow—possibly to get clear of the American who'd bet him till he had a plausible bargaining-line—the man scuttled to the entrance, set perhaps on rustling up a body or two to hunt for the Voice of Grenada. Someone seemed already up for it, bulking briefly in the entrance, making in the direction of the lobby doors. That bulk...the lobby...when first we came in...I was again minded to check it out, but 'Ladies, gentlemen, ladies, gentleman' swung me back at the stage.

Robbie. He didn't drop a stitch at the jug-man's desertion. His grin mirrored Ambrose's and, from the edge of the stage, he raked the resettling punters with it. You'd think that, with his renewed welcome, he was saying that the whole Esp thing was a set-up. Some kind of wacky, huh? But that's how we're minded to let our evenings roll on the Isle of Spice. Lob in a firecracker or two, you get me? Role-play and stuff. It was masterly. Right then and there, I'd have written a testimonial to make him top man of the island.

The grins, the vamping chords, they did the trick. People now sat confidently back in their seats as, once more, the lights dimmed. Esp's lady-fans commenced a sway-shouldered transfer of affection to Robbie and Twinko's big brother. The claimed knight, Robbie thanked the sirens politely and slid offstage. The Americans resumed their places among their countrymen but opted to fold arms and give Ambrose a cold, dead stare. The chords flowed on, the beats rolled round them. Presently, the arms unfolded; a buddy was sent for fresh drinks. Seconds later, I was summoned to the stage, handed the makeshift claves. My nonplussed expression further relaxed the crowd; soon after came the whistles of jokey encouragement. I didn't care. The flight through the windows, the footsteps, the soft thud. That could have been me bailing out on the Voice of Grenada, keen to make distance, impatient with just walking. I'd hardly got the first few taps in when Eric came back, joining us on Ambrose's far side. *Follow me,* nodded Ambrose again, to the neck of Eric's guitar.

He'd kept his ears open, Ambrose, all that while in Caracas. I recognised some *gaita*,[39] songs about cuckolds and incontinent pigs whose gist he translated with roguish delicacy. Others told of protest, tyranny, stories of blood or freedom. Yet others were lighter, salsa-y, about how good it feels when the breeze of evening is on your face and the right woman is in your heart. What Twinko said about Eric back in the *Mirabeau* was spot-on. He was surely good. He and Ambrose struck big sparks off each other. That's what I remember now: the guitars, Ambrose's unaffected voice, light and mellow, a pace that found itself without effort. Wisely, aside from the brief translations here and there, Ambrose didn't dally between songs. Nor did he throw in anyone's idea of a greatest hit. All that belonged with the previous hours, the bizarre entertainment they'd offered. As we flowed on, you might almost say that those hours belonged to some other night, to someone's embroidered fancy in idle talk of life's worst moments.

Dark now. The pillars and foliage seemed to suck in

---

[39] Gaita: a style of folk music from Maracaibo.

the low lighting, leaving us in comfortable gloom. Clapping swelled and faded. We took it in turns to swig from the drinks that Robbie ferried up. The front-row ladies beamed equally on us all: bliss all round afterwards, maybe. Now and then Ambrose taught everyone a chorus, nodding and grinning at them when their turn came as though even the raggedest effort did right by the song.

'Hey, Santana!' cried one of the Americans when, unexpectedly, I found myself embroiled in a sticks-and-conga break with Twinko. Another voice cried that he knew this producer-guy in Philly.

'Like Santana's the drummer,' muttered Twinko. 'Fucking ignorance.' But I thought he should check out the Philly cry. For myself, at the very least, I could imagine doing some almost nifty tap-tapping back over the water, back at the campus folk-club, perhaps behind someone's run at 'Don't Worry, Be Happy' or such. I smiled down at Robbie, who looked even happier than when convinced Esp was really playing ball. He hadn't gone looking for the jug-man, couldn't care less, it seemed, where he was.

'OK?' I mouthed.

His answering twinkle was what I bring first to mind if I want to recall the evening in shades of gold.

Of course, some folk gooned about. The sound of certain lyrics struck them as odd or worth punting as a joke, so we had this and that cried at us. Others lobbed in the usual chestnuts, *Islan' in dee sun* along with *Dayyy—o!* and *dayli' come* (fair comment: night was wearing on). *A-wimoweh* made its long-service appearance. Fair play, though, they were considerate enough to try and insert the stuff in rhythm and key with Ambrose. Well, most did: *a-wimoweh* gave someone trouble.

The flow, good humour, blonde prospects, even the Americans singing and clapping along. We got underway with another, and it had just occurred to me that I might get some folding money for this when *a-wimoweh* stuttered in again. Ambrose's voice broke on a laugh and we all chuckled:

'Sorry, folks,' he trilled out, 'not quite the groove for *wimowehs* on this, ok?'

There were some indulgent smiles, as though we'd just done the private-onstage-joke bit. Ambrose shrugged:

'No mind, we won't come embarrassing whoever.' Pleasant bemusement at this. A few folk looked round for the miscreant.

On we went. Just at the second-time chorus, a mighty affair about the Manzanares River, *a-wimoweh* broke out again, now sounding rather toneless. More chuckles from us, Twinko going one-handed, shading his eyes, making a big show of gawping about. More bemusement from below. Robbie starting away, patrolling the tables, halting midway up the room. Third-time chorus cantering up—the joys and woes of corn-pounding—and *a-wimoweh* louder, emphatically toneless and the penny dropping that it wasn't coming from in front of us and Robbie shrieking and running forward, all of us turning round, the French windows ajar, the foliage jostled, the form in the gloaming, the raised arm, the gun shiny.

The slap on the thigh with the gun-less hand, a rhythm slow and ugly. The voice incantatory, scarce-human. The gun rock-steady as though the words were smoking from the barrel, words about our greatest national convulsion, words whose way was pointed, it seems now, right from that day when it was agreed that too much was being asked of 'contraband':

Yankee fuck the Grenadines, 'tober '83,
Yankee row the boat ashore, 'tober '83,
fuck my girl with a pistol-butt,
island in the sun
fuck my world with rocket-shape dick
island in the sun
bullet from our masters
shrapnel for my dame
Yankee row the boat ashore
island in the sun.
Yankee mother-fuckery—sledgehammer—nut!
Yankee mother-fuckery—sledgehammer—nut!
Bullet go fly round sick—house,
Mad—house, poor—house
Bullet go fly round your house
Make like a bird like a cracker up you ass!
Yankee fuck the...

Answering cries and howls from the floor of the *Alhambra*. Hey, these Yankees had flown ashore in good faith. This here now is vacation, asshole. Maybe sun, fun and night-moves didn't make the profoundest mission but it wasn't the most wrong-headed either. I watched their convulsions. They weren't here for post-invasion roughhouse and, at the least estimate, they'd soon be gone, leaving tips and card details behind them. My enemy then is my consumer now—it's tough, messy, hard at times to figure, impossible even. Yes, some of them might have had family in the contingent that set its foot down hard on our land in October '83; some might even have been here back then. For enough Grenadians, the scar was only just skinning over. And yes, at another time, in another mood, I might have cheered Esp on. But, chou poule, he'd given us arseness enough, messing up a good thing for Twinko and Robbie if no one else, and now here he was and that gun wasn't shaking the slightest. This wasn't protest. Any rightness about it was coming out of a whole heap of wrongness and there was no point, now, trying to understand that, even if a body wanted to. All you could say for sure was he'd messed on his own stoop. Ours.

A move. Twinko. This was it. I tried a block, Ambrose lunged, but it was no good. Twinko shook us off and advanced on the barrel. The look on his face made me foolishly glad that he hadn't thought to retrieve the bird-knife after it zinged past him. At least this way…oh Lord, this way what?

'Fuck you, Belmar!'

'Oh, daddy.' Robbie cried out for all of us. Stripped of his romantic names, busted back to the school register, Esp wouldn't hold his pose for the satisfaction of his vengeful drummer. There were statues enough in the room; and I felt that, near or far, all saw the finger curling to the trigger like on a city-park movie screen. I sensed, too, that there were more of us now, a new commotion at the back of the room. Ambrose leapt…

…arms wove in shadow around Esp's chest and arms, a bullet ripped into the floor before the gun bounced and Eric darted to retrieve it.

'No, no,' said Ambrose, 'prints, prints.' He gasped for breath there on his beam end, knowing about as much as the rest of us about who or what had put him down. The shadowy arms slithered up to Esp's neck and he was hoicked out through the windows. A moment later they were clicked shut. Twinko took a step or two further and stopped dead, shaking.

'Cops?' said Eric, gesturing at the windows. But before anyone could speak, 'Hey, hey!' and the little jug-man was at Robbie's side. 'What you at?' At first it sounded like managerial chagrin at an evening damaged, revived, utterly destroyed. But then I wondered if …no…seriously? Had he registered nothing of what had just happened? Did he think that, even now, there was life in his bet? Was whoever had Esp in that neck-lock a heavy who'd been tasked with keeping the boy shooter in view, thus corroborating the flimsy idea that, see, he'd been with them all the time, in spirit anyways, see? And had the heavy been so drunk on success that he'd screwed up the plan? Something like this must have struck Eric, who came down off the stage, pushed Robbie gently aside and leaned down to the jug-man.

'He had a gun. He fired a gun.'

'We pupa,[40] you all still standing.'

---

[40] An exclamation of disgust.

Ambrose joined them, pulling Robbie back in place, holding hard to his shoulder.

'Ain't you just recent fatigue this one for the eruption? Didn't he get you out of the kaka-pul with his compere chat and we taking stage right with him?'[41]

'Aw, no, no, no-no.' The jug-man started wriggling away. His manner suggested they were pressing him on something which wasn't the issue right now. But we saw what it was when, nerving himself up as best he could, he beckoned to one of the Americans—all of them still motionless—and squirmed up more space between himself and Ambrose. The American slowly detached himself as if roused from cryogenic slumber, at which the jug-man started nodding, rubbing his hands. He mouthed urgently as the American approached. The American's expression changed from a hawkish intent to disbelief.

'I do? Me? I owe you?'

'Sir, please, lis', lis' to me.' Reaching, the jug-man wrested Robbie from Ambrose and tried to use him like a shield.

'My colleague, sir, lis', my colleague here, he see that the silly madass never lef' the stage, all the time in the foliage, sir, lis', playing games with us—'

'Get off!' Elbowing himself free, Robbie pushed his face into the jug-man's. 'You don't give a damn about this place!'

'And the gun, compadre?' The American was about an arm's length from the jug-man's quiver and sweat.

---

[41] Kaka-pul: foul shit.

109

'Blank, sir, blankety-blank.'

'You fucking little shitass.' Esp, the American reminded me of right then, his voice a slow grind, as though he were yielding again to an ice-sleep. 'He left, left—no finale, no bitter end, so get me my fucking money before— '

A double-slam, shaking the glass near out of the French windows as they flew open. Now I had to grab Twinko to hold him in place. Swinging him down beside his brother, I caught the jug-man taking off with the American in pursuit through the crowd, now swelled with what that far-back commotion had promised: other guests, more management—and now two policemen pushing through. Some prophetic soul must have got onto them, I guess, around the time Esp started that Yankee stuff. I swung back, confronted this time with the Voice himself, willowy and spent at the very back of the stage, looking like a marionette in the instant the string-man lets go. He'd maybe thought to get clear of his assailant but his legs had said no can do. Or he'd been waggishly planted onstage as a morality exhibit, *Foolery Unmasked, Hubris Defeated* or some such. Whatever, his time back on the boards wasn't long. A bull of a shadow grew behind his shoulders. A spread hand reached round and I expected to hear that weird compere from *Cabaret* hiss *'Ladeez and Gentlemen, your own, your very own Voice of Grrrenada!'* Nothing. But at once I was all over sick. Dim the lights might still have been but I knew that hand, its gesture. Next minute it tightened at Esp's neck, dragging his yelps back into the dark again. I dared not think what had happened already out there.

The policemen flew past us, one scooping up the gun with a rag, rushed at the windows, stopped dead. What was it about the back of the stage? Twinko had stalled on his way there too. But I knew already. Between the windows, that hand declared itself. Delayed by all these months, the exchange we never heard on that school afternoon found voice for us at last from out in the dark:

'Say my names! Give me my names!'

'Mr Belmar, you simply—'

'No Belmar, never Belmar, you give no notice to that asswipe Twinko.'

'Mr Belmar you simply do not have it. Never then, never now.'

'So why you round all the yard-gigs? Why you weave shoulder in big crowds? You love what I do. Why won't you let self say it?'

'Me, Mr Belmar? Me in a crowd? Weaving?'

'I will go to a foreign land,' screamed Esp.

'It pants for your arrival, Mr Belmar.'

'Where no-body—*nobody*—can contraband.'

'Gentlemen'—the hand that had released our compositions to us so often, so disdainfully, beckoned to the policemen, breaking their respectful ex-pupil freeze, and pushed Esp forward. The policemen slid out, going either side of the marionette, and shut the windows behind them.

There was enough authority in the room—other managers or guests used to lording it in their everyday lives—to clear most everyone away. The lady-fans left in a huddle. Perhaps love had been tough on them in the past and they'd decided, understandably, that this was

111

another kind of tough they didn't need. The Japanese party exited with heads bowed, the ladies weeping; one of them gave a trademark sigh as if signing off from the whole schemozzle. That left us, jumping as one at a cry of despairing pain from out in the lobby.

'That's him,' chuckled Robbie, mimicking the little jug-nods, the rubbing hands. 'Getting his.'

'And him?' Eric pointed to the windows. 'Esp?'

No one moved. You might have thought that, even after all, we felt some concern. Maybe we did but no one betrayed it. I think we were all just grateful to be right there, well past knife and gun. More curious than obligated, I started moving to the windows, only to be stopped by a double-glower from Twinko and Ambrose, big bro with both arms around little bro as if to soothe him after he'd stumbled on an ant-hill. Eric stirred, crossing the stage right into that dead-spot that had spooked Twinko and the cops. He hung irresolute, shoulders drooped, not like him any time. A bright light flashed up and melted across the windows. The cop-car reversing? Esp's terrible angel ostentatiously flashlighting his way home, job done?

'They'll be gone by now,' covered Robbie. I met his eyes, their light snuffed by ruination. Turning aside, he started, the first to see we weren't the only ones left.

Chairs were scraped aside to make a wide gulley between the tables. They came in a ragged patrol across the room, feet dragging as if in surf. Twice Esp had flummoxed them. Their passion wasn't going to lie down now:

'You guys'—slow, slow again, the menace of the

words, the same way their buddy had faced the jug-man down. Breaking off, the head American worked his shoulders; a pal dealt with an obstructive chair, which bounced once and rattled the glasses on the un-Moorish bar.

'You guys are all the same. Can't keep yourselves together. Couldn't get laid in a whorehouse.' The feet came on. 'Your buddy needs a whupping and you know it and you knew it and still you let him fuck around. Ha? We set aside good time and money for him and it's pissed away. Ha? He won't get nothing will he? Slap on the wrists and, hey, sorry you lost your piece, here's another, don't kill too many, you hear? Ha? Lucky that other guy took him down—only fucker with any sense of right in this whole shit-pile. Well, let me tell you something, my friends, we have money enough between us to pay for damage and raise bail and bribe ourselves the fuck off this island. So here we go with our own little massacree….'

Pound, pound, pound. Our feet synching with our hearts, going off beat, getting it back. I'll never be that good a drummer for real. Bits of the picture come back to mind now but never the whole thing, I never got it. The French windows; Ambrose, a guitar; Eric, a guitar; Twinko, djembe under his arm like he had a burst-suitcase-train-moving-off thing going; Robbie and me either end of the conga, funeral clowns shipping a coffin from wrong church to right church. We didn't stop till we got somewhere far and hidden from the teeniest wink of the *Galaxie* sign. No steps behind. Waiting, looking one to the other. Still no steps. And we set down the stuff and stretched and felt our levels drop and recovered the average thump of our hearts. And realised we were right by Duttine's Cooler.

I stepped a little way out from its shuttered dark. Twinko did, Eric and Robbie did. Ambrose stayed sat and in a bit, maybe for the hell, quietly strummed a chord or two, I think from that song Esp broke up with his *a-wimowehs*. The chords fitted right in. Because it wasn't that very moment any more: it was long ago, an afternoon hot as all get-out, and there we were, waiting, buzzed now and then by old man Duttine offering a pallet, a plug of ice. Waiting again in that desert scene in a movie where someone comes at you slow and you can't tell if what you see is a living form or a trick of the shimmer. Maybe we all hoped—despite, despite—that the American ba-john was right and there'd just been a slap on the wrists and Headey and our Nowherian had gone their ways, enjoined by the cops never to meet again and miraculously agreeing—agreeing also to disagree. Maybe that hope was our last snatch of loyalty to the boy who gave us The Rock Exponents, The 'Ponents, and could hardly let them go; gave us contraband and never let it go at all.

'I could do with a plug of ice,' I remember murmuring that afternoon. But now colour was coming, day-birds were starting up. Through the non-shimmer, a human form kept on not showing…

…and kept on ever after. We never saw or heard. There

were rumours of a stretch in Richmond Hill,[42] quickly superseded by stronger ones of removal off-island. The Belmars vanished. In a curious twist, their house was taken over by one of Eric's crew, about to exchange rings and settle down.

Robbie of course did likewise. Got another job and another, better and better, till he became a head manager, fronting the biggest hotel on the island. I'm godfather to his second.

There was a sighting back in East Park, Caracas, but no one confirmed it and maybe, after all, it was just someone who'd seen Esp when Ambrose did and was so struck aside by him that he thought anyone acting goofy there must be Our Nowherian and no other.

Eric returned to Germany at that summer's end, Uncle Padmore's plaudits in his ears, endorsements from the section boss in his suitcase. Studied, lectured, advised—at last fulfilled Uncle's prediction, that night in St George's hospital, that the Bundestag would be snookered without him.

Restless Headey retired in a puff of smoke and shifted elsewhere: Port of Spain,[43] this body said; Castries,[44] said another. Another other said, no, Florida, which just couldn't be: in our lessons he'd done enough berating of the Disneyfied world, which he held responsible for our stubborn illiteracy. Still, a colleague of Uncle Padmore's, in Key West for some US-Caribbean junket, swore he'd

---

[42] Richmond Hill: Grenada's only prison.
[43] Capital of Trinidad and Tobago.
[44] Capital of St. Lucia.

115

seen him down in Mallory Square. Seen them both, yes, man and boy side by side, waiting with everyone else for the sun to dip below the water and bring on the nightly party.

Twinko's never off a cruise ship these days. His band, I hear, is mighty and money has made the sweetest love to him. Don't take my word: check out the feedback on the cruise-line website. You want Marley? You got him. Hey, you want Ray Conniff, Mel Torme? Just wait on that mai-tai, settle back, sip it slow. And, boy, that singer the drummer's got. His brother, you know? Spent some time in Venezuela, got a passel of folky stuff from there. Man, he does this one about how good it is when the breeze of evening is on your face and the right woman is in your heart. I swear, the whole ship stops what it's doing when he's onto that. I'd say the captain drops anchor even when there's nothing to drop to. For sure others'll back me up. Come on, folks, leave a happy comment.

The website messengers are mainly American: some kind of rapprochement, you might say, to make up for *La Galaxie Bleue*.

Some other body says, no, no-no, Esp's in Richmond Hill, all right, special unit, and he ain't coming out or allowed visitors and his folks'll get the call when ashes-to-ashes time comes but that's it.

I saw my father come back hale and sober from Montego Bay that summer. The family shaped itself lovingly round him—even Rosa, who took it on herself to prepare him 'nutritionous' breakfasts and oversee his enjoyment of same. I swung a job for a few weeks as a gofer at Gorgeous Grenadine 396 Radio up in Sauteurs, crashing with Marieve , RW and the kids and never once seeing any evidence to confirm Mother's notion of RW as a long thin streak of devilish sloth. Dammit, he put in the word for me at Gorgeous Grenadine—and all round Sauteurs and beyond his word counted. At summer's end I went back, north-west to Eric's north-east, saw out my time to the tune of 'Cold enough for ya?' and earned my own Nowherian stripes in this and that locale. Finally I ended up here, in England, sort of like that Paddy on the Railway pitching up on the Liverpool shore.[45] In the brief spell before my England job started, I toured about a little; checked out Bilston, Roseville, that gas appliance place that claimed time Uncle Padmore would never get back. A retail castle now—beds and car-phones and interactive doo-dads.

Uncle Padmore—leave him sing 'Paddy on the Railway' once at a family fete, he'll drive you nuts with it all the night.

Some other body said Esp took his life.

---

[45] 'Paddy On The Railway', a traditional Irish song.

12

7, Coneygreane Place, Hagley.

Some other other body says, '*Woo-woo, woo-woo.*'

Thelma from next door. If she'd said nothing, I'd still know her loiter, like a space-displacing scent. I set down the letter and find her in the kitchen—offer her coffee, but she has to crack on. The pie she slides onto the counter is piping hot:

'Rhubarb,' she says—then, voice dropping, 'might be a bit too sugary. Sorry, love'—dropping more—'Harold plays his face at too much sugar.'

I thank her, assuring her that 'too sugary' has never been a problem.

'Summer Fete this afternoon,' she adds. 'Blakedown. They even say the rain'll knock off. You should pop along, love. Stalls and games—Olde Englishe things.' Nudging me, she twinkles. 'Go on, have a giggle at the Morris Men. Daft buggers.'

Back in the living room, I sit and look over the envelope: the conference of stamps and redirections, the blocky writing, the extra 's' to my name. Delaying, I get up and head back to the kitchen, make another coffee, cut a slice of the pie—which, like everything Thelma brings round, is perfect. Take my time.

Seated again, I start re-reading. The writing itself isn't blocky but neat: something of the amanuensis about it, someone tasked with after-the-fact formality—as though the address was the last and only thing the sender could rise to. I imagine my mother's verdict: 'So after all this time he never manage a postcard direct at all, he get some

118

other body on the job.' I try to put her aside but, as is her wont, she fights a while: 'Didn't I say the *Galaxie* thing would go catastrophous? Ah-sah, that poor mad husk of creation.' I try again, getting her to shut up after her murmur of 'rest, rest, peace, peace.' Again I read the life from that moment when he materialised through those French windows and hung before me in a blip of freedom before those arms, that hand, repossessed him. All these years, all the letter's redirections: the story could be contraband itself.

I have a feel for how to ease through the letter now. I blank *by the time you read this* whenever it appears.

The End

Tickle, Tickle
A novella

I have this world. Slip into it when I want to. I've no idea how and I can't remember when I found it. I imagine it behind the bookcase near the bed, open all hours as the saying goes. So I can get there in a jiffy. Out from under the covers, quick slide over the books and there I am. The seasons are faithful there, stay put like they should. Always late summer when I'm outside that old church with the wall full of ivy. Winter when I stand at the gate to that huge wide field and step forward, just a little way, no further. The gate's never shut as far as I know. Held open, it is, by something in a sack. Could be big stones, though I think I've spotted a screw-cap. A can, then, full of stuff that you need on a farm but has gone out of date. Not oil or petrol, I'd say. Think of the risk, however long it's been standing. Even I wouldn't do something as daft as that, leave flammables out in the open, and I've been daft enough in my time.

I'm there a lot, at the gate, in winter. Always arrive just as the first snow falls. The flakes dip about like butterflies over the grey earth, then the earth sucks them in. Who knows, they might have been real butterflies once, they might have flown to the field from the grasses round that old church. I couldn't say. Actually, it'd have to be further back than late summer for butterflies. Wouldn't it? And I'm never outside the church before the last of August.

But the field's my favourite. Me off down behind the bookcase, standing by the sack. Silence. Bit of wind sometimes, though, bit of a creak from the latch-end of the gate. And somewhere far away, his nibs, turning a little in his sleep, flinging out an arm, muttering though he swears he doesn't. Because I'm there too, of course, beside him, even when I'm not.

I say I have this world. Had, really. But I might again.

Fatal, maybe, saying about the field and the church to Trish. But that's Friday evenings for you, the extra bottle, the two-for-one job, the shame-to-waste-it looks going back and forth. Like it wouldn't keep. But I told her and she said it was fantastic, I should write it down. I didn't want to write it down. I was scared that if I did it'd vanish, I'd lose my sense of it, it'd be like pushing a pin through one of those off-season butterflies, watching it crumble in a glass case. That's how I felt then, anyway, so I mumbled something, the usual, not one for words, not fussed about writing in school. Anyway, they're not about words, the field, the old church, the gate and the ivy. They're about being there, knowing they're there even if you close your eyes, especially when you do, maybe.

Fair's fair, Trish didn't press it, that's not her way, bless her. If she thinks she's buttonholing she steps back, says something more general, so you don't feel on the spot. The buttonholing is still in there, I suppose, but it's, you know, tucked in, part of her wider tack. I knew what was coming. She cracks open the two-for-one bottle, the one we didn't need except it was Friday evening, what the hell, and says OK, but I should still come along, I'd really enjoy it.

I read. Easy reads, mostly, some would call them.

Thrillers are a big thing but the old-fashioned kind, country house weekends, murders in Mayfair, detectives stuffing pipes or knocking them out on their shoes. Not the modern ones, the strong meat stuff, set in Swedish wasteland as likely as not. If I see adverts for them on platforms, I start shivering, not just because of what's probably inside them but because of the feel they give off. Hot day in mid-July and those ads can still make me feel like I'm stuck in my own fridge. The snow on my field, that's quite different. A friendly cold and much of the time I hardly notice it.

Sometimes, too, I'll have a yen for something seasonal. Christmas I'll have a go at one of Dickens' stories. Summer, Laurie Lee. I've even dipped into a poem or two at Easter. Devotional, you'd say, certainly old, sixteen-hundreds. Is that sixteenth century? I always have to think when I try and match those up, the century, the hundreds. Gives me a funny feeling, reading them. I don't understand a lot about them but I imagine standing behind the poet, quiet-like so as not to disturb, while he's writing and crossing out, trying again, getting it right. I can almost hear *Aha!* when that happens, hear the quill, I suppose it'd be, going mad across that dusty paper. Some people say they admire such-and-such when what they mean is, I've less than half a clue what it's about but there it is, it's finished and complete, someone put in the time on it. I suppose that's how I admire the Easter folk, the scratchers and crossers-out. They wanted to get somewhere, writing. Like I love arriving at that open gate.

I never figured Trish for a reader. Well, it doesn't come up on Friday nights. Indirectly, maybe, sometimes.

122

She might ask if I've seen such-and-such on TV and I might say, that was a book, I think, to start with, and more often than not she just does that thing people sometimes do with a glass to their lips, a flick of the head to say, well, fancy, and then back to what Friday nights are for. Loves song lyrics, though, Trish. Fastens onto what she likes and can't understand it if you don't. Loves classic stuff. Roy Orbison, *In Dreams*. Had it played at her wedding, even though I said, and I wasn't alone, look, it doesn't work out well, that song, there's no woman there with him, no dream-girl come true. She said it didn't matter, and anyway, there is because he's thinking of her, singing of her, making her real. Life isn't always how it appears, she says, even in a song. Procol Harum, *A Whiter Shade of Pale,* that's another big fave and, all right, it's pleasant but don't tell me the words mean a thing. She won't have that. Poetry, she says it is, though it's about as far as you can throw from what my quill-merchants ever came up with.

Maybe that was what did it. Her idea of what poetry is, plus her never-ending hunt for groups and clubs, which I can't blame her for, her bloke being all sorted and scheduled with his interests, hence the Friday evenings, the bottles of two-for-one. Anyway, she saw a notice, might have been in a supermarket entrance, even a library, who knows, somewhere with stuff about adult courses, volunteering, self-help. This bunch of writers, alternate Wednesdays, centre of town, an old hall, I know the place, just about keeping on its feet with ping-pong and old-time dance, talks on this and that. So off she trots. She's been a few times. Awoken her, she says it has.

Surprised her. Surprised me, a word like 'awoken' on her lips. Started writing poems and found she was full of them. So yes, I daresay all those song lyrics made her think she'd have a go at scratching and crossing out and trying again, if she does all that, if they don't just pop up, which by the sound of it they do. You should come along, says she again, the Friday after she first said it, or maybe the one after that, with the bottle on the tilt and that broad happy grin. You'd love it, she says. I had tried asking to hear one of her poems, even part of one. I mean it's great that she's found this in herself, all power to her. But she wouldn't, not even helped by the far end of the second bottle. Then it was, okay, you'll hear if you come along. I should have expected that, probably did. She wouldn't want me not to hear but now she had this gentle Friday-night leverage. I know her of old.

Finally I did go, sort of. We'd arranged a drink in town for when she was done so I just slipped in the back at the end and waited. I'd never been in there before though I must have passed it scores of times. Dismal old place, it is. You'd need to be drunk on words. Kind of place that, as soon as you go in, you think it must have started raining, you wait for the spatter on the panes. Bit of a stage at one end, fol-de-rols either side, leftovers from some jubilee, Victoria's, I shouldn't wonder. Door on the left into one of those kitchens that doesn't want you to bother with it.

I said I slipped in at the end. Another bit of Trish mischief. Six-thirty to eight, she said, but it was gone eight-thirty when it broke up, I had words later, teasing really but still. So I found myself sitting through the three

124

last turns. An old chap in a paisley cravat read a bit from his memoir. He was nice, a looker in his time, I'd say, only his face was thin and collapsed now, his voice wavered and he sometimes had a rest-up in the middle of a word. A work-in-progress, he called it, and by the look of him I'd say it was a race between the two of them. The bit he read was about Dauntless Dougie, an uncle I think, or godfather, a padre in a war, the First I suppose, though I didn't recognise any of the place names he mentioned but maybe it was the way he said them. Bit of a character, Dougie. Got the men to pray with him in little groups and then slipped them big goes of rum from his secret store. Told them a nip of that on Calvary and Christ would have been down from the cross and making short work of the guards, which isn't the kind of message you expect from a man of the cloth or, come to that, his nephew or godson in the kind of hall Christ might just rush into.

Then it was Trish and I have to say, she was good. Poem about finding herself following an old lady round the supermarket aisles, just coincidentally, watching what she dropped into her basket and picturing what the things said about her, where she'd come from, where she'd go after the check-out. A Life In Perishables, she called it and it didn't rhyme, which was a surprise, what with her and Roy Orbison and Procul Harum and what-have-you.

Last up was a young girl with what she called a dialogue of trespass, between her and the wounds of self-harm. Everyone got a bit uncomfortable at that. The motherly-looking sort next to her kept furtively looking

125

her over as she read, trying to see if it was autobiographical, I suppose. But she didn't seem the type. Blonde hair and drapey blouse. Could have done with a square meal but nothing strung out about her, as you might say. But then, what is the type? The motherly sort, who looked and sounded like she led the group, asked her straight up once she'd finished, but the girl said no, it came out of things she'd read, a documentary she'd seen. She didn't talk like round here. Student, I thought, which was half-right because Trish said later she'd started and abandoned a degree, which is more than I've ever abandoned. Rolled that one round her tongue, Trish did—'abandoned'. Like 'awoken'. It was funny, really, seeing your best friend in a new place and saying things in a new way, like half of you is rooting for her and the other half doesn't know her at all. 'In go the peas,' her poem about the old woman said, 'and she's back at the long, long trestles in a Wiltshire street, tee-bar sandals and diluted squash and cheering and Churchill all over the air.' Sight better than sixteen vestal virgins hoofing off for the coast.

When they broke up I headed for Trish with my cod-daggers look. Finish at eight on the dot, my eye. That's when I saw a figure on the far side of the hall. Waiting for someone else, I assumed, apart from which, I had to admire his brass neck. Togged up like the cravat gentleman might have been when he chatted with Dauntless Dougie way back when. I thought he might have been a manager of one of those retro shops, ration-book chic from war-torn Blighty. I couldn't see his face but that was no surprise. Probably less than a half-dozen lights in the place and three of them were round the writers' table. But he didn't come to claim anyone and after I'd got to the table and Trish had done that blurry introductions bit, all those names and no hope of remembering, I looked round and he'd gone.

Fair do's, Trish didn't announce that I wanted to join. But naturally, when we were in the bar, she asked what I thought of it, meaning her. To which I asked who the hand-me-down bloke was hanging about in the gloaming and she said what bloke? Oh well, I said, never mind, and he got lost in the chat, me telling her how impressed I was with her poem, her raising an eyebrow and saying, well, how about coming for the whole thing next time, then me raising my glass and assuring her I'd need several of these inside me to so much as consider it, and her laughing and the chat going elsewhere.

Only on the bus home did the bloke come back into my mind. I wondered if there was some themed thing on after the writers, a charity-shop jamboree, and he was early for that. I'd have thought it was pushing it, squeezing another event in that evening. Then again, hall like that, they need all sorts in, maybe even get special late licences. It has to keep going somehow. One of those jumpers, the bloke was wearing, greyish, different colour edging to the vee. Dad used to wear something like, no shape to them at all, Mum was always on at him to get rid of them, so he would, well, get rid of one, but another one just the same would take its place. Odd, really. She always took him clothes-shopping so he must have got them on the quiet to snape her. I wondered if they were made ready-shapeless, like drip-dry. Georgie and me, we'd dig each other's ribs when he came to the table in the latest, then Mum would get in between him and us, leaning extra low to put out the food, mouthing at us to shut our yap before it started, but you could tell that she was quivering, you could see her twinkle, how she swallowed the laughs I'll never know, except I do, all composure she was. Later on I imagined her taking herself off now and then to somewhere quiet, a forest or something, so she could spend the whole day hooting her socks off at a lifetime's idiocy from Dad.

It's about fifty yards. You get off the bus, into our avenue, the Bartons' first on the left with that saggy side-fence they'll never replace no matter what they keep saying, then us. Always someone about, a neighbour, dog-walker, but that night there could have been a cast of thousands and it wouldn't have made a peck of difference. Something was at me as I got off the bus. Behind me? Around me? All I know is, I legged it like a greyhound, straight round the side of the house, too, no faffing with the front door because I knew he'd be up and the back door'd be open. Just at the back I stopped, thought of Mum, got myself composed. Listened. Nothing. I wondered if the drink had got to me, cheaper than usual that night it was, probably a dodgy off-load, nothing to do with special midweek offers. Of course his nibs didn't notice anything. I love him dearly but, if shapeless vee-necks were still the thing…it took me a dog's age to wean him off those sky-blue tracky bottoms. Superior lounge-wear, the sales bloke had told him. Those folk, they see him coming.

That night I got myself to my open gate. Stole away

128

upon the midnight, I suppose I'd say if I was a quill-merchant or even, maybe, in one of Trish's poems. The gate was shut and the sack was gone. The field looked as though some giant badgers had been at it, heaps here, gouges there. The snow-butterflies came dipping and weaving but they didn't fade into the earth as normal. A blizzard came on, proper fierce, fistfuls of it, and swallowed them up. And the cold…nothing friendly about that, not like I knew before. I felt like a human thermometer with the mercury plunging, I felt like I'd been thrown in the sea on New Year's Eve. Shook my arms and legs, not a ha'porth of difference. I stepped back and nearly went over on an ankle: another deep hole, must have opened up while I was standing there, and the sack that should have propped the gate open was half-buried in it. Stuff this, I thought, where's August, where's my old church? But it was snowing there, too, back-end of summer covered in white and the ivy had been half-dragged off the church wall and the wall was skewed fit to tumble. And never a leaf on all the trees in the churchyard, no, just one clump on one branch, and a little bird dancing this way and that, trying to stay hidden behind the clump like the snow had made it too scared to fly and all it could do was hop and let its wings go useless.

What could I do but get away? I tried to cry myself to sleep and I might have got an hour. The rest was him twisting, muttering. I got a shove to the back of the head at one point. I remembered the girl from the writing group, the student as was with all that chat, her and her self-harm going back and forth. A dialogue of trespass, she'd called the thing. I felt I'd turned into a trespasser in my own world, except maybe it wasn't mine, never had been, and I was like a kid who could play somewhere only because no one notices, because everyone's forgotten wherever it is, till they remember and move in with their big signs, their fences, their snow, and shoo the kid off. But no…this was my world, just as it was, you might say, the kid's proper place. Finders keepers. But that hadn't stopped something from being what it was and doing what it did. Because apparently it could.

Couple of days after, I was late home. Customer looking for some special turmeric they'd heard we'd just got in but could I find it? Could I find any of the spices and stuff? That's that new manager, can't be more than fourteen, head full of changes, must have got the night-stackers to switch everything around on the dry food aisles just for the hell of it, and of course a queue as long as your arm when I got back and Julie hopping about too, waiting to take over the till and then of course she forgets her code and the person after the turmeric says, actually, this isn't really what I want so I spit invisible nails while I'm seeing to his other stuff and then his phone goes and he paces about while his stuff piles up on the belt and then it's, actually, do you have a couple of bags? So I sort him out and see him off by which time Maureen's poled up with Julie's code so that's all right at least and I go sloping off with the turmeric and find I can't find where I found it till that nice new woman on the deli counter comes out and helps and we locate its context as that kid of a manager would say and then when the deli woman gets back she finds she's got a queue out the door and her weigh scales won't display properly but luckily Maureen's just dealt with someone at the express counter shouting the odds about a lottery ticket he'd bought last week and the express is just round the corner from the deli so she nips out and gets the deli woman sorted, honestly, Maureen should be running the whole place not some toddler brought in over everyone's heads.

So it was gone six-thirty when I got through the door and he says Mrs Barton's been round. So I thought, oh, right, they're seeing to that fence at last, want us to move our stuff away from the boundary, in which case why hasn't he done it? Fifteen, twenty minutes' work? Alright, it was getting dark but everything looked to be where it was when I came in and him working at home that afternoon, phoning and computing and insuring away. Flexi-schedule, he's got, which is all very nice but sometimes I could flex his neck, dishes still piled up from our breakfast and his lunch, stuff still lying about. Just occasionally he'll have a mad tidy-up like one day's heavy industry is quite enough for the whole month.

But it wasn't that. On the hall table, he says, adding that I was lucky, Mrs B was just going out that morning, a couple more minutes and they'd have taken it back to the depot, which is the other side of town, car or two buses. No card through our door, mind, telling us. And the Bartons might have been busy for days or put it down somewhere and clean forgotten, and I'm not hot on telepathy, nor is he, however much he can make his numbers dance on his screen. Bulky, it was, properly padded, a row of stamps, maple leaf here, profile of Queenie there, Charlottetown postcode on a white strip,

131

with 'Prince Edward Island: Canada's Ocean Playground'. Our address all neat on the front, sender's address all neat in the top left corner. Always partic about her writing, Georgie. Well, she married someone with a partic life, flight lieutenant on some exchange thing at Brize Norton, draughtsman originally, then re-trained after he'd whisked her away over the water and finished his time, went into landscaping and cabin design, well, they're big on all that over there, they've got the space. And it is lovely, where they are. Anne of Green Gumboils, Georgie calls herself, says her eldest coined it, well on the way, he is, just finished whatever they have to do, articling and such, and got snapped up by a law firm in Ottawa. Makes up for their girl, I suppose, though, God bless her, she can't help it, who knows what demons can get in your head? Has her own little place at the back of their house, goes out with her mum now and then but that's about it.

Mind you, our Christopher looked to be going that way in his last year at uni but then the exams came and went and he turned himself right side out again, which was a mercy, though that's not what his sister said. Too much of those dates and battles and kings and priests, she says, enough to send anyone off the deep end, he needs to get back in the now, she says, be a grown-up. It's West Hampstead, Mum, she kept telling me, Borough of Camden, all because I told folk it was Camden Town when she moved. Wash my mouth out. Town house, she calls it. You could fit three of them into ours, just about, and ours is no palace. Something in management, she is, which could mean anything from director of Selfridge's to what Maureen does at our place. Human-facing, apparently. She and our kid of a manager would get on no messing. Never goes into details, likes to keep it impressively mysterious. Hang 'Em Flog 'Em Rachel, his nibs calls her. Don't you ever let her hear you saying that, I tell him, though of course he's the only one who could get away with it, with his little chuckle and nod of the head.

The sad thing is, though, she'd probably grin and look all cat-with-cream if he said it. I don't know what's happened. She's just gone very hard and I don't know why, it isn't as if she's had any more knocks than most as far as I know. Marriage is out, she's said so. Flings, I think she has, nothing that lasts, a few weeks, a couple of months and pfff, it's over. She seems to take pleasure in that, like making best friends in school just to duff them up. Brought a couple of victims here for visits, nice lads, he took to them, up the pub and that, but she laid out the eggshells round them, slightest thing and she bit off their heads. Maybe that's what you've got to be seen to do in human-facing management. No way to live, taking your work home like that. Laughed like a drain when I told her our Chris was going on to a Master's, all funded, mind, some History council or group or something, well, he's bright. What, she says, he's putting himself in for more punishment? Has to go down to London now and then, he does, British Library, archives and that. Phones her for a drink. Never convenient.

I thought I'd scan these and email them to Brainiac— Georgie's time-honoured name for his nibs *—but* *that's not the same. They're all copies and I've been promising. I still don't know how I ended up with most of them. I was thinking we could divvy them up last time you were here but I guess the trip down to Nova Scotia put paid to that sister-time we'd been hoping for. Then I just forgot and you seemed easy either way about it. But finally I told myself, this is no good, so I freed up some time— Richie was away on a job over to Cape Breton—and I hope you like the result. Say hi to Brainiac for me, give that Chris a huge aunty-hug and tell Rachel I hope some prime catch sweeps her off her feet before she can open her mouth. Just kidding, kind of. Miss you everso, Helen. Get yourselves back over here. Love and love, the Gumboil One xxxxxx. PS. Crazy no-shape jumpers galore inside. See how many you can count.*

The album was really plush, and Georgie had gone to town on the packing, not a dent anywhere. All nicely presented inside, that sticky plastic smoothed down over each photo, I can never manage that, the ruckle queen, me, or I couldn't when I had actual photos, he saves everything on files and disks now, keeps promising to get hard copies done, dream on, I tell myself, dream on. Chronological, too, by the looks of it, soup to nuts as Richie the cabin-man would say. But I didn't have time then for a good shufti, it was Friday evening and I needed to have a bite and change or Trish'd be sending out the bloodhounds. I phoned her to say I'd be running late and she said if I'm not completely starving don't worry, she'd got enough for a scrumptious party-tea, which sounds like it'll pitch up in one of her poems if it hasn't already, so I splashed a bit of water here and there and got on

134

some comfy old mis-matches and, hoopla, his nibs said he'd give me a lift over and taxi fare back and it didn't even cross my mind to say, alright, who is she? We were just reversing when I remembered and leapt out and grabbed that wine off the kitchen counter, our kid of a manager's choice for some autumn promotion, and it's pretty good, a tasty Australian red, Vasse something, with a bouquet that does all sorts, not that it dawdles in my mouth long enough to oblige, Trish's neither, still, fair do's to the toddler for choosing it, maybe he's not completely useless Eustace.

And Trish had a red to match and I couldn't fault her party-tea, so it was a happy evening after all the turmeric kerfuffle. I think I might have even said I'd go along to her next writers' do without her having to do her grin and top-up routine. Never crossed my mind, my churned-up field or my churchyard with that little bird scared to death among the bare branches. Or that bloke all shadowy at the side of that cave of a hall. At some point I think I pictured myself turning the pages of Georgie's special album one by one, finding what she'd put where, seeing it all in right order. But yet another top-up must have carried that away.

Saturday's his training. Well, not his but the shivering bunch in the youth team that he's assistant coach for. Been doing it for years, though he could barely run twenty yards now to make a useful delivery or collection or whatever those herberts call them on the Saturday night tv round-up. Mind you, he admits it. I've met the coach, northerner, played for Accrington Stanley back in the day or nearly did, or his brother did and he was in the reserves, his nibs gave me chapter and verse but it slid off as quick as a mouthful of that Vasse. Hot on the offside rule, apparently, the coach, which probably means about as hot as my determination not to understand it.

So, house to myself and the Saturday morning ritual, phone call to Chris, who sounded under par, to be honest, though over the years I've weaned myself off the third degree about proper food and exercise and giving his eyes a rest. Nice flat he's got himself, right near the Bristol campus, sharing with an Indian lad, physics or maths, I can't remember, Naagpal, only Chris calls him Nag which is a bit disrespectful but he's a whizz with the food, his nibs and me, we eat like royalty when we visit, so you're Nag, I said, first time we met him, well I hope you're nagging him to stay off the burgers and chips, and Nag, Nagpaal I really should say, he laughs fit to burst and says please be assured so, he talks so nice, better than most English people, better than me. Then I called Rachel, which of course was just the answerphone, well, who'd know where she was and who with, so I left the usual, all well here, hope you are too, phone when you can, love from us. His nibs keeps threatening to leave her a message all spooky-foreign, *Rachel, thees ees your consheeience speeeking*, wish he would, she'd phone back like a shot and tick him off in that giggly way she has, like I say, he can get away with stuff. She does phone, once in a while, between important things, all breathless and sorry-gotta-go, usually to tip us off about a forthcoming northern progress, as he calls it. I suggested we should just go down sometime, unannounced, but he gave me an on-your-head-be-it look. I just hope she never has another conquest in tow so I don't have to feel what the poor bloke's going through.

After all that, a cuppa and the album. Wine-red, the cover, which tied in nicely with last night at Trish's. And there it all was as I turned the pages, me and Georgie from when we were kids, and Mum and Dad and cousins and uncles and aunts and best friends and Christmases and holidays and rubbish hairstyles and clothes, ours as much as anyone's.

At one point I stopped and looked over Georgie's note and thought a bit but I couldn't remember either how she'd ended up with all these photos, two of each into the bargain. Mind you, she did come back to help with the house after Mum and Dad passed, Dad then Mum that is, about a year between, but I was focused on the bigger stuff, probate and such, putting the house on the market, well, I was local so it made sense. So stuff like photos, non-probate, so to speak, I didn't pay much attention to. Like she said, I must have been easy either way about things like that, and she'd brought a couple of whopping suitcases and hardly any clothes and I could imagine Richie and her kids, no, not them, they'd have been far too young at the time, I could imagine Richie telling her that he wanted a real feel for her life before they met, well, they're big on all that over there, where people come from, loved ones or the last generation or the one before that, all that interest in the old country, whichever one it happens to be, and he'd said to me once, us and the Americans, we're all orphans when you get down to it. Anything you can bring back, I could imagine him saying, I'd love it. Dearly love it, that's his phrase, beautiful voice he has.

It was funny, going page by page, I mean nice-funny not odd, or I suppose I do. A life coming back like a trick of invisible ink, oh, look, that's what it says here, that's what it says there. It's not the whole story, I know that, but I felt tempted more than once to close the album and lift it on the palms of my hands and say, here's me as was, I'm as red as that Vasse Trish and me made short work of and I'm this wide and this deep. I could have thought, blimey, is this it? but the trouble Georgie had gone to ruled that out because her tidiness was really saying, look, it was all worth taking care of.

Each photo had a neat little sticker. I could remember the details in bits and bobs but not how she'd managed it, if she'd remembered it all, maybe not, maybe she'd gone on some site and found our family, Your Ancestry or Remember When? or however they're called. I can imagine Richie encouraging her that way, gently telling her to do a thorough job, his partic-ness meeting hers, telling her to remember that she and me weren't like him or the Yanks, orphans. The stickers made me feel like I'd come out of a coma, or awoken as poet-y Trish would say, and things were dropping into place in their own good time. So that was how the garden looked at Merriman Rise in 1958, with the swing (I think I could just about remember it) and the cold-frame (I couldn't). And that dog, more Georgie's than mine, less hers than Dad's, called Sputnik (I didn't remember) not Dusty (I did but he was two dogs and four pages later). Comical effort, Sputnik, mongrel, a Heinz 57 job as Dad said, well, they all were, though Dusty was almost sort of a Border

138

collie, sharp muzzle like they have, like I think they have, a sweetie he was. As for Dad's shapeless wonders, Georgie was right, I counted five in those home photos before I was three pages in.

It was good to get the holidays lined up. So Rhyl was 1960 not 1961, which was Dawlish which I thought was 1964 but that was Majorca, how could I have forgotten the year for that? Big to-do, injections and new shorts and cozzies and the passport rigmarole and Georgie and me giggling at the photographers and Mum hissing what-for at us and us almost behaving and then Georgie whispering shouldn't there be an aspidistra behind us? and both of us in a heap again. Shame the photos can't show all of that instead of the four of us looking awkward outside that hotel, 'Mimosa', the sticker says, 'Cas Catala', or Mum looking petrified with the sea-water round her ankles, or me and Georgie in those shorts, mine stripes, hers plaid-y, mind you, we thought we were the goods, and Georgie was, or nearly, already getting a feel of what was what, boys trailing after her, getting their eyeful, so much so that Mum gave them a piece of her mind once, I remember that, then rooted in her bag for a towel and threw it over sis. Big dark thumping silence from Georgie after that and I was meant to take her part, solidarity, unspoken, but I thought it was funny, plus I was probably jealous that I wasn't old enough to be almost the goods in the way she almost was, so I got the mardy treatment from her too, a good couple of days it lasted. Dad was oblivious to it all, of course. Spent a lot of his time trying to perfect that thing where you pour wine from a tight spout onto the bridge of your nose and it runs down and

139

you push out your lower lip and catch it, all the folk in the bodega egging him on, local regulars, those pop-up holiday pals you always get, specially in pubs, ruined three shirts he did, I remember that, and I remember the hotel manageress sucking her teeth, eyes like saucers, and gesturing that the laundry'd have the devil's own job with them.

At least the shapeless wonders were nowhere to be seen at Rhyl or Dawlish or Cas Catala. But they were back on Dad with a vengeance for all the Christmases, even with stars and reindeer in 1967 ('Larkspur Road, just moved' said Georgie's sticker) and we were into colour by then so they looked even more gruesome. A moment of Dad-madness, that camera, I remember, with Mum going on about how the cost of it would put us on the parish. Then the work photos started popping up among the gardens and dogs and tinsel, headed by a close-up of an invoice, which seemed all odd and modern, the kind of thing someone would get it in the neck for wasting film on back then but at least saved Georgie a sticker. *Wm. Mostyn, Electrics and Mechanics* and the Larkspur Road address and the number of our first phone without a party line. Electrics and Mechanics. Mum, that would have been. Dad would've been happy with *Car or Lights up the Spout? I'll sort it.* Then a big house the sticker says was out Church Stretton way, 1968 (Georgie must have done some proper digging, or Richie) and Dad by a ladder with a jazzy-coloured shapeless in full sail, must've blown his overalls apart. He got a lot of work like that, I remember, old mansions in need of rewiring, new monstrosities where he had to go from scratch, always

140

broke his heart that he couldn't get in on the council estate scene but big firms had the dibs there. Similar snap for Monmouth, same year, only the shapeless was bright green and the sticker said 'Family excursion', so he must have been doing a job near Uncle Dai and Auntie Eva and we all piled down together. That would have been not long before Georgie left home with her secretarials and got that job at Carterton. No idea why he had work photos taken, in situ as our kid of a manager would say, unless someone told him it'd be good to build up a stock and show them round, like you'd have on a website now. I can just imagine how flummoxed he'd be, confronted with a website, he was impressed from the off that his nibs knew his way round personal computers when we got that first one, 1984 or 5, must have been. Commodore, was it? Apple? He'd ask his nibs to go through something, whatever computers could do back then, and just stare while he did it. Yes, I'd say someone told Dad to get a bunch of photos round him, 'Me and my work', probably a bloke in a pub, treated drinking pals like Moses with his tablets, he did.

I went to turn the next page having a quiet bet with myself. A Fairisle shapeless coming up? Something in manky yellow? But two pages stuck together and as I was about to run my finger down the edge the phone rang and I dropped the album on a chair and it was his nibs saying he'd be back later than usual because the head coach had some news about a change of ground for their lot and other teams that had been on the cards for ages and he wanted to talk it through. When I got back the pages had unstuck themselves and were open on the chair. Four photos over the both of them but I only saw one, a pub bar with a bunch of faces in the background and two to the fore: *Seven Stars,* the sticker said, *New Year's 1969, Dad and his apprentice, Alex??* It was the only sticker in the whole album that was short on firm detail. Two questions marks must have meant Georgie was proper flummoxed. But it didn't matter. I knew. After all this time, I remembered with knobs on.

I stood stock still and sipped at my tea. Lukewarm by then and I'd usually pop it in the microwave but I didn't bother, I hardly noticed. Then I got my coat and went out for a walk that got longer each time I thought of turning back, all round the estate and up to the by-pass, along the cycle-paths and through the little short-cuts. I remembered that the nice new deli-counter woman lived somewhere near, on the part of the estate that's all wild flowers, Trefoil Close, Willowherb Rise and such and I was pretty sure she was on Bluebell whatever it is and I know she's got one of those Smart cars so I thought, find Bluebell and a lemony shoebox-y car and I could call in but then I thought, no, she told me she always signs up for weekends to fill the time, hubby's away a lot, metals rep or something, one son in Carlisle, another at uni, daughter in the Signals Regiment or maybe that's the Carlisle son, still, it'd be nice to have a cup and a chat with her sometime, I'll ask her when we're not having to hunt the aisles for something's flaming context. So when I felt I had to turn back, when I pictured the last of my tea all cold and scummy in the cup, I went round by the playing fields and watched the kids. Mainly toddlers with at least one parent, a rare old time on the swings, or primary kids on the climbing frames. But some were older, getting on for the age I'd have been when Dad watched the birdie in the Seven Stars on New Year's.

Alex Kinsella, his apprentice. With Dad about, what, four, five months by then? Two considerations brought him on the scene. Mum's words, two considerations, and sure as eggs it was Mum's notion and she wouldn't back down till Dad saw the sense of it, which he soon did. For one, he wasn't getting any younger and for two, wasn't there some grant or such he could get for training a lad up? (Of course there was: she'd done her homework.) Perhaps the idea was that any lad would sort of take over and Dad would become less pressed, the side partner but still senior on the invoices, and yes, Mostyn and Kinsella would have had a ring to it, only it turned out it wouldn't be Alex, he devilled off a few months after that Seven Stars photo and Dad soldiered on alone but with smaller local jobs, enough to see him through and not so far to travel, well, the big houses were drying up smartly by then though he did get a lot of flat conversion stuff, steady earners, and some pals helped him out on the car side, cash in hand, they weren't as crackers about rules and regs back then. Actually it was May 1969 when Alex went. Long enough before my school exams that I was able to concentrate. I wouldn't have otherwise.

Scouser, Alex, though you'd have been forgiven for thinking he was a bloke with a Scouse part in a play or on telly and couldn't get it quite natural. Overdid it, too many 'fabs' and 'gears' and all that had gone out by then, it wasn't the Mersey Sound any more, it wasn't the start

143

of the decade, the Beatles were getting a bit strange, I bought that White Album and Dad said, waste of money as he'd done for years to Georgie and me but this time I mainly agreed though I'd never say it, well, you wouldn't, parents and kids, the unwritten rule, 'Honey Pie' was nice, though, and 'Blackbird', and George's 'Weepy Guitar' or whatever its full name is got me weeping along with it but as for stuff like 'Don't Pass Me By', best to stay sat at the back, Ringo. And of course I can't listen to 'Dear Prudence'.

But Alex traded on all of that and lots of folk still loved the Beatles enough that he did all right with the girls as far as Dad's hints about it went, elliptical intimations his nibs would call them and maybe one day one or two such will surface in a Trish poem. The girls. His own age or round about. Which he bloody well should have stuck with. Maybe one or two of them could have tried drumming some with-it dress sense into him for when he was clocked off and in civvies. Maybe some of them did but I think he was pushing the Scouse thing again, the Beatles, how they looked around the time of 'Penny Lane', and anyway Carnaby Street was still coining it then, the Regency look, the idea that all oldies were natty dressers. So if he came round or went out with us, and it happened a fair bit thanks to Mum the clucking hen, poor lad far from home, square meals needed, he looked like a mini-version of how Dad's dad must have turned himself out for his courting days. With Dad's fatal weakness thrown in, too, though Alex's shapeless wonders at least looked like they might have had some design to them once. And as I stood and watched the kids on the fields, I realised. I pictured the one he was wearing three nights before, there in the shadows at the side of that grim old hall. Positively spruce, what I could see of it. Of him. Because it was him, sidling back to me through time, standing, waiting. And waiting when I got off the bus and got my Olympic gold racing for the house. Loved the waiting, Alex did, loved his shadows. Loved that he just knew I'd never say.

I took it slow from the playing fields back to home, thinking, if I can just run it all through before I get to the front door, maybe it'll all be gone, done like a dose of salts by the time I'm washing my cup and starting to think about our tea. Daft hope for something that's been biding its time but you hang onto things like that, don't you, like when you're a kid playing hop-skip and thinking if I miss the cracks in the pavement I won't die. So I kept hoping as I left the kids further and further behind because I couldn't not.

All please-and-thank-you Alex was when he came for a meal or met up with us wherever it was, the Legion or a pub where I could be parked with a Vimto in what they called a children's room, honestly, some of the other kids I passed my evenings with, you'd shudder. I was at that odd age, I suppose, too young to go out on my own, too young to stay in alone of a night, wouldn't have been so bad if Georgie had still been at home but then nothing would've. I went over to friends but their folks were much the same, none too happy at the idea of girls unwatched of an evening and as for staying over, well, you can imagine all that was stacked up against that, school nights, other stuff on at weekends, the faff of arrangements and a lot of my friends' folks either didn't have a car or their dads were out or back at some ungodly hour, like mine often was, so it would have been all too difficult for pick-ups and drop-offs. So if we were going out I could go over to a friend's for an hour or so but then I had to be back and scrubbed up for the Legion and the Vimto. I was at a stuck age in a stuck time, you might say, no wriggle room as our kid of a manager declares if you ask why a display has to be right here and not somewhere where folk don't have to dance round it when they're in a rush.

Always helped me with the wash-up, Alex, if he had a meal with us, always ferrying Vimtos or lemonades to me in those smelly pub rooms. That's how they start, I suppose, taking chances, feeling out how much time they have, figuring how it could be stretched a bit more and a bit more. Finding out stuff, too, like once in some pub when he came in with yet another awful Vimto I asked if they had Coca-Cola, forlorn hope but I wanted to show I wasn't keen to end up made of cheap pop and he twinkled and said, Coca-Cola? Ooh, Prudence, Prudence, you're not in Majorca now and I'd never mentioned that holiday to him, I'd mentioned nothing but he must have done some nosing when he was with Dad and not only about Majorca, it turned out, he had all sorts up his sleeve, my birthday, how I used to go a bundle on tee-bar sandals when I was a kid, that I'd bought the White Album. I could have throttled him then, in that pub room because after he'd gone the other kids fell about thinking my name was Prudence.

He started early with that name. I'd lay the table for

the evening meal and go upstairs to wash my hands and he wouldn't be there when I went up but he would be when I came down, it was like he knew, like he'd been watching the house for a bit of movement at the landing window and made his guess and rang the doorbell. So when I came down it was Mum with well, look who's called, like she couldn't have known, like she hadn't made enough for four, and he'd twinkle and say, ah, dear Prudence, and stretch out the 'dear' like a sarky rhyme for sneer.

Full of chat he was during the meal, work things with Dad, who clearly thought Mum's apprentice idea had paid off in spades, compliments galore on the food for Mum who needless to say thought he was the bee's knees from the off. Not so full of chat when he was with me for the wash-up, not at the start anyway. Made out like he'd been struck shy which wouldn't have fooled anyone and shouldn't have fooled me but what could I do one way or the other? There I was, washing up, an agreed chore like with a thousand other kids at that time, like you'd get a contract and write where it says 'your signature here'. I could hear Mum and Dad in the living room, Dad riffling the paper or faffing with the telly though Mum would say, honestly, Will, not with a visitor, and then her tapping and clinking, fetching the Drambuie or the Tia Maria or the Double Diamond out from that tiny little almost posh bar they'd put in the corner of the room because she said it reminded her of the one in the corner of the dining-room at that hotel in Dawlish. And Alex on the drying up, real slow, five goings-over with each thing till you could see your face in it, even the ones you couldn't have anyway.

School, he started with on his first visit, how's all that, then? I said what I liked and what I didn't and he said that was just like he was, Geography, loved it, French, for the birds, Art, what was the point? Everything an agreement, like Rachel and the way she used to drive Chris mad sometimes when he'd be trying to talk and she'd repeat the last few words of all he said. Then there was an outing to one of Dad's awful watering-holes and in came the Vimto with some crack about how budding geographers needed a clear head and this stuff would sort me out. Next time he was round and I found myself becoming Prudence, it was school again and I immediately thought of the Science lessons, the labs, all that writing down, what we did, what we observed, what we concluded. Method and evidence. Try it now, I told myself. So when he asked how the studies were going I said, thinking about it, if there's one thing I can't stand it's Geography, and he said that could have been him speaking, what do you need to know beyond your own world and your own place in it? I love Art, though, I said and he said Art was gear and if there was one thing he loved it was a good painting, like the ones you saw in Woolworth's, a Spanish donkey or a woman with a jug on her head. I had it in mind to say I love Maths and I hate it but what further proof did I need of his caper?

Then on the next expedition to a pub he came bearing the sacred Vimto and saying something about it was for the dusky lady's jug, which made one of the other kids ask if he was mental and he said, no, just in love and they giggled and one pointed at me and said, Christ, not with

148

her? and he just twinkled and vanished and left me to face them, if I'd said Christ out loud in public it would have been Mum's hand at the back of my head.

Same with boys. So who do you fancy? he said at our first wash-up, making long, long work of a side-plate and I'd say no one and he flicked my arm with the cloth and said, ah, go on, bet you do. Next time I had someone at the ready, well, two people in one, Neil Hughes a couple of years above me who was really nice and good at sport and Graham Bentley who was in my year and a whizz at Art, so I mixed them together but I didn't give a name, I thought it best not to. But even as I was talking about him, well, them as him, I thought I might have been saying too much and I was right or I guessed I was, well, I was sure I was from the way that he reacted. A look like thunder then like dismay and then kind of sorrowful. He could have been Mrs Appleby, our sort of head of girls, the one you were meant to go to if you were having private problems, not that they were private for long, mouth like Blackpool Tunnel she had.

Now, he says, I was just funning when I asked you before, but, Prudence, you're far too young, there'll be time enough for all that, boys and such, and won't you know it. Then it was like he shut his face up and the thunder vanished with the rest and he twinkled and said, I won't breathe a word and nodded his head back towards the living-room, where the paper was rattling and the glasses were tinkling their way out from behind the bar. And it was like Mum and Dad were twenty miles away, even though I could hear them, and each time after, when he took as long as God's beard with the crockery,

149

it was like they were another twenty miles off again.

I can see now. I can see it's all grist to the mill. You say you like this and then say you don't, you say you fancy a boy and then say you don't, you say anything at all, and they'll say, well, that's what she told me, her being all butter-wouldn't-melt, playing games, leading on.

And of course the other stuff started early and kept pace with the rest. Tickle, tickle, Prudence, he'd say, and I knew we were done with just words. The flick of the cloth became a flick across the chest which became a hand on the arm which became a nudge of the leg which finally became a finger. Now Prudence, don't you be thinking about the other boys. But it wasn't particular boys he meant, not even the boys in my year or our street, no, he was pushing the very idea of them into the shadows, getting himself out front. Like I say, he loved his shadows. And the finger would travel and soon enough a mate joined it. Tickle, tickle. I remembered when Georgie visited one time, just after she'd met Richie, and I overheard her and Mum having a good old giggle over what Richie said about how the blokes on the base would try it on with the local girls ('But not him' Georgie said, more than once) and about how, in Richie's words, the blokes had Roman hands and Russian fingers. Alex's roamed and rushed, all right. It probably excited him, the notion of Mum and Dad only a couple of doors away, but then again he was a fast worker all round, because one time Mum came in for something and his hand was back round the cloth round a saucer in a trice.

First time I was struck all of a heap and stop it, stop it was on the tip of my tongue but it never came out and I tried to move away but he moved too and I moved again but I could only do it so much because after that I'd have had to climb onto the draining-board. Same game the times after and he'd keep the chat going and somehow so would I because I thought, maybe there'll be a last question and I'll give the last right answer and he'll just stop. Or maybe he'll think I can't feel him, that I'm making like there's not enough for him to be felt, and he'll throw down the cloth and go in and tell Mum and Dad, lovely meal, thanks ever so, but I have to go and he'll tell his mates that his gaffer's daughter's a real ice maiden and get roaming and rushing elsewhere. But saying stop would have stopped nothing. I tried thinking of Neil Hughes and how I wouldn't mind him doing all that but then I thought, no, I don't want anyone doing that, not just yet, maybe not ever. I asked Mum if I could wear my jeans for the next visit but she said not on your nelly, guests for a meal means doing things properly. I thought of speaking to Mrs Appleby but that would have meant a whole school hooting and falling about like the kids in that smelly room when he called me Prudence.

So I just stood there. God help me, I just did. And it was a blessed relief any time a visit coincided with Georgie coming home for a day or two off. Those times he'd give the lot a quick spit and polish and be out of the kitchen before you could say, well, Woolworth's donkey. Maybe he thought at least there's me to fall back on if no headway was forthcoming with her, which there wouldn't be, because quite apart from the fact of Richie we were all in the hall one time saying our goodnights to Alex, and Georgie turned away behind Mum and Dad and caught my eye and rolled hers. And then she inevitably brought Richie over and Dad must have told Alex and invited him too but then he reported back and it was, sorry, no show from the lad this time, he says an old friend's passing through. But that didn't throw him for other visits. Finally he got his finger in. Tickle, tickle. A dead awkward angle and I didn't help by not moving. Some might call it standing your ground, not giving him the satisfaction of a response, but it was nothing to do with thinking, it wasn't another school lab experiment. How can you think when you're frozen and scared and all alone? When the nearest to thought you can get is to feel that it must be happening to someone else a million miles away and somehow it's got mixed up with you right there with a spoon in your hand? Scraped his bloody nail getting in and his nails weren't like a film star's, that's for sure, I'd have thought Mum would have noticed and had a quiet word with Dad about that but maybe she thought, mucky nails, honest toil and let it go.

Stung like billy-o, it did. No, more than that. You can draw a sting and the red goes. It was like he'd emptied me out and that finger was the whole size of me. Then there was Mum's voice in the hall and she was opening and closing the cabinet with the phone on top and saying, well if it isn't here I'm blessed if I know where it would be. Out comes the finger and he dunks it in the suds like I was dirt on it. That's it then, I thought, hoped, when I came back to myself, he's hit his target for now, please God forever. Silly sod, me. But in fact he didn't turn up for a while after that, nor at the pubs, and Mum and Dad didn't mind overmuch because there was Mr O'Byrne to think about.

I could say it was Mr O'Byrne's fault, what happened after, and I did think it at the time, but even then I knew it was daft. The O'Byrnes lived across the street and along a bit and Mr O'Byrne had a clerical job but he was a dab hand at all sorts and got to helping Dad out with the car repairs. A miracle-worker, Dad called him, on account of being round there one day and watching him take a mantel-clock to complete bits, even the gilt off the casing, which of course was Dad all over, his love of exaggeration, but still, everything came out and was arranged perfectly on a newspaper and Mr O'Byrne cleaned and oiled each bit like you'd bathe a baby (Dad again) and put it all back together sweet as a nut. Not one piece left over, not a screw or spring, which in Dad's view separated Mr O'Byrne from every other fiddler and fettler on the planet, himself included. Dad said he was a cut above, that he had a saint's touch, which was more than exaggeration, actually a bit poetical for him, but that was perhaps the result of exposure to Mr O'Byrne's patter, the old blarney.

Whenever Mr O'Byrne came round and saw me, he'd start on with some old Irish song, 'Saint Theresa of the Roses', only he'd change it to Helena, or 'She Moved Through the Fair', which he never sang all the way through except the once, him and Dad coming back from the pub one summer's night, everyone's windows open, till Mrs O'Byrne collared him at their garden gate with 'I'll be moving ye through the fair in a box, ye goon.' Lovely voice, he had, though not for gone eleven of a weeknight in the street.

Mrs O'Byrne made the loveliest deep pancakes, hot cakes she called them, and insisted we all call her Caitlin. Older than Mum and Dad, they were, and I think they had one of each but they'd left home an age before.

Then Mr O'Byrne retired and out of the blue they were packing up. Going home as Caitlin put it. Westport, home was, County Mayo. They kept in touch, though, and Mum and Dad said more than once that a holiday over there was on the cards. But then it wasn't because Caitlin phoned one night sometime after Alex had fetched up on the scene and the next thing was that Mum and Dad were dusting off their mourning wear and arranging for me to be farmed out to Mrs Pooley, a widow two houses down. Very end of April 1969, that was, and Mum and Dad had decided that it wouldn't be seemly just to go for Mr O'B's funeral and shoot straight back so I suppose you could say that they got an Irish holiday of sorts. Anyway, a week they were gone, and it was half-way through the week, the Spring bank holiday Monday, in fact, that I remembered I didn't have my gym kit for next day. The house was all locked up but I had a key. Mrs Pooley offered to come back with me, like it was a hundred miles away, but she probably had visions of me waltzing back with the front door still wide open. Bless her. I could have said yes.

And I could say it was my gym kit's fault. Well, it could have helped by being where I thought it was, or in the second most likely place, or third or fourth. But what am I saying except it was my fault really? Hark at me, pinning it on myself. That's all part and parcel, though, isn't it? You think it's all down to you. If you'd been here not there, if such-and-such hadn't happened then but a bit before or a bit after. But it isn't all that, it's what Richie calls it, dumb luck. Anyway, I wasn't all that untidy then, unlike Georgie, who created clothes-bombs all over the place, so you'd think things would be simpler now she'd gone. But the kit wasn't in its usual drawer or in the one above or the one to the side or the wardrobe. By then I was into the where-did-you-last-see-it? bit where you try and think clearly but know that from then on you'll just go dipping in any old place. I wondered if Mum had put it in with some of her stuff by mistake, which wasn't likely, and I wasn't keen on riffling through her smalls and hangers but I gave it a go. No joy, of course, though at least I had enough presence of mind to get her things looking as I'd found them.

I should have looked in the scullery soon as I came in because that's where Mum kept the stuff-for-the-iron basket but I was sure as sure the kit was ready and put away because Mum had got me into the way of ironing my school stuff and I was convinced I had. I nearly didn't look there, I was heading for the door with some lame excuse forming for Miss Aldridge, our tartar of a PE teacher, when 'scullery' popped into my head and chased out the realisation that I'd left the front door ajar in my rush, so instead of shutting it I nipped round the corner of the kitchen door and sure enough there was a pile of stuff in the ironing basket, well, you couldn't blame Mum, all the preparations for Ireland, she'd had her hands full and decided that whatever was in the basket would keep. Not too much in there but I could see an arm of my gym-blouse hanging out and I found the skirt just under. My pumps were lined up in the hall so I suppose at some point I must have told myself to remember to take my kit to Mrs Pooley's but anyway, job done at last, and I remember having a quick look through the living-room window as I headed for the front door and thinking, oh, sun's going, could be rain but it's only a short sprint to Mrs P's if it comes on. And I remember I'd put all the kit in a Mac Fisheries bag, the only one I could find, and it didn't smell of fish at all but the very name made you think it would, or should, but again, I thought, no distance to Mrs P's, she'll have a better bag because she swore by that new Tesco's that had opened near us.

Late afternoon it was by then, going on five, and I thought, any minute now I'll see Mrs P at the front door checking all was well. But she'd probably gone out in her garden when I said I'd be ok, especially if this was the last of the sun, toast of the street her garden was, neighbours helped when they could, Dad sorted a rockery for her. Funny what you remember. Funny what glues itself to a time and a place.

When the cravat gentleman in Trish's group read about Dauntless Dougie, his uncle or godfather, there was one bit where he said Dougie could throw his cassock over his head, shoot his cuffs and scoop up his prayer book in one unbroken move. Like a running tide, he said the man was. That was pretty much the way of it when I checked I had the house keys and reached to pull open the front door—the door pushed wide, me knocked off balance, the Mac Fisheries bag flying, the door shut, my kit on the floor, his voice saying, ah, thought you'd dress up special for me, nice, nice, me dragged along the living-room carpet kicking and pummelling, then his hand on my face, other hand clamping my legs, my head banging against the corner of the little bar, stuff clinking and rattling, him pulling and grunting, me trying to lift and punch, his hand down double-hard on my mouth, the chill where my knickers had been, his knees squashing the inside of my legs, me with no help in the world, him sort of in, tears in my eyes and my stomach on fire, him in for certain, me bone dry, his johnny like rubber cable, me splitting in bits, him slobbering, me scared and mad and scared and mad and his hand like a vice but me still trying to get the screams out, for Mum, for Dad, for Georgie, still squeaking their names against his bony fingers, his long man-cry like I'd actually been one big bloody disappointment, the weight off, the no-knickers chill again, my eyes tight shut, the sound of stumbling, something bumped into, a quick 'oh, fuck me', the front door slammed.

I lay there for an age. All I could think of was how disgraceful it was, me with my knickers down in our living-room, me almost damaging the little bar that Mum had set her heart on ever since she saw the spit of it in the corner of the dining-room at that hotel in Dawlish. Then I got up and, slow as a snail, moved but couldn't feel myself, watched but couldn't feel my hands as they got me together, folded my gym stuff and put it back in the Mac Fisheries bag, checked that nothing was broken in the little bar. Watched but couldn't feel my feet as they got me from here to there, smoothed down the pile of the carpet, got me round to what Alex had stumbled into, the hall cabinet. Watched but couldn't feel my hands again as they pushed it back against the wall and put the phone right and checked that all was tidy inside, as first one hand then the other went to the back of my head where it had hit the corner of the bar. Waited, as you might say, for them to tell me it was wet there, sticky, or a bruise was starting.

Nothing, my hands said. But there could have been everything. How would I know with feeling gone? Of course I checked and re-checked a score of times later, angled my hand-mirror in front of the mirror in the room Mrs P had put me in. Just a bit of tenderness and a throbbing that was gone by the night. That was luck at least. Thank God for thick hair.

Like I thought, Mrs P was in her garden when I got back. I lifted the bag and managed a thumbs-up and she called that there were some Tesco bags behind the kitchen door if I wanted something roomier. I sort of nodded because blood was on my mind again and I should have checked earlier but I just wanted to get away from the house and a few seconds later I was sat on the edge of her bath with my knickers off and loo roll at the ready. I hadn't felt anything but then I wouldn't have, running back to beat the band, to get in safe at Mrs P's before my legs gave way. A mercy that there was just spotting, well, I say just, there was one ugly dark patch but at least it wasn't a river, still, that was those knickers gone for a burton so I rolled them up tight as tight and put them in the Mac Fisheries bag to get rid of on the way to school. Mrs P called up that she was just popping to see Mrs Maidment, another lonely lady, widow for longer than Mrs P, a bit younger too, according to Mum, but Mrs P was like a spring chicken compared to Mrs M which was why she looked in now and then to see if there was anything Mrs M wanted. Steak and kidney pie and veg when she got back, she called, so could I set the table?

I got myself sorted as best I could and went to sit on the bed. Finding things weren't a calamity down there started to bring feeling back properly. And thinking. Of course he knew Mum and Dad were away. Dad would have genned him up on their current jobs and probably let slip that I wouldn't be going. At a neighbour's, I could hear him saying in his airy, hail-fellow way, few doors down, and just as well—what's the betting our Helen'll have to nip back for something? Her own head, as like as not.

And so he'd been sort of waiting, maybe all weekend, blending in like some spy, watching like he seemed to watch the landing window when he came round for meals. Ah, there she goes, I imagined him saying at those times, there's my Prudence on the landing, and his ring of the bell would be full of what I'd had dished out that afternoon.

Downstairs I laid the table extra-neat like that was something I could put between me and the afternoon. I thought of some of the girls in my class, old campaigners they were, even at that age, talking at lunchtimes about when they'd had it and who with. I'd say sometimes they'd got caught like me but they were fly beyond their years and I'll bet they turned it around, took control. I tried to imagine talking to myself that way, tricking

159

myself into the cool and easy, oh yes, me too. Tried to place all that alongside the neatness of the knives and forks, the glasses and the squash, another bit of distance. I knew it wouldn't work but it kept my mind busy. Well, they got exactly what they wanted, those girls, which wasn't the sharp corner of a bar and bloody knickers in a Mac Fisheries bag.

Marathon tomorrow, is it? Mrs P asked when we were eating and I smiled and said long jump and sprints, weather permitting. She started on about what they had to wear when she was a girl, PT they called it, near enough boots and overcoat compared to what girls could wear now. But netball was her favourite, she said, and she wasn't half bad though she said it herself. Nifty at tennis, too, fancied herself as another Helen Wills Moody, whoever she was. I was glad she was off on one. All I had to do was nod now and then and say, yes, lovely pie. The rest of the time I was like when the telly shut down at night and you just had that high-pitched noise. Just at one point I wondered if I'd got everything as it should be in the hall cabinet. But that was it.

I knew exactly what he was banking on and I didn't disappoint. I told no one. By the time Mum and Dad came back I'd pieced myself together, so to speak, as the girl they'd said goodbye to. It was a sight harder back then, coming out and saying, not like with the girls today though it costs them dear enough, poor scraps. I suppose I imagined the worst if I tried to say. Dad was out of the question, though I loved him a bundle and I'd called for him with the others against that bony hand. Mum would be tender and horrified but maybe the horror wouldn't all go where it should. I could imagine her reminding me at some point of the time I'd wanted to wear jeans for an Alex meal, seeing that in a new light. Oh, yes, wants to show off what's coming, wants to be like big sis. Maybe a score of other little things would add themselves to that and bring her to a verdict. I'd been hurt but I'd been stupid and the stupid trumped the hurt. Plus there'd be, now don't you tell a soul, which would be all about shame and I felt that as it was, plenty of it, far more than spots on a pair of knickers. Georgie would have been the best bet in other circumstances but she was gone, she wasn't in my world any more, she was all her job and Richie and the big life. And anyway, she might have taken her own version of Mum's line, which, God knows, I've taken enough with Rachel. Giving off vibes, they say now, though she'd have had her own words. Were you trying something on without knowing it, Helen? Making out something you hadn't a clue you were making out?

What could I have said to that? What are you supposed to do? Lock yourself away? And anyway, I wasn't, I know I wasn't. I didn't ask for him to be at the dishcloth. I didn't beg for the finger. So yes, I imagined the worst if I tried to say, but maybe too that was a way of protecting myself from what I felt I just couldn't do anyway. Say it out loud. Find the words that didn't in any way make me sound like a tease or a scrubber. I wondered what Alex was imagining. Nothing much, I guessed, except that he'd scored but I was a bit of a crap shag so he'd have to gild the lily when he and his mates got into bragging.

Chris used to have this daft little game with his

soldiers. For ages there was a hole in the hallway skirting board round where a heating-pipe came down. His nibs finally sorted it but till then Chris used to set up his battles there, his offensives, and the side that lost a soldier down the hole lost the whole war. Except that he made sure he never lost one because it was all about symbolism, notional loss, his words, he'd swallowed his dictionary by then. So a soldier's head over the hole meant peril for that side but shoulders over meant defeat and no messing. One time, though, a soldier landed half-and-half, like that van on the cliff at the end of *The Italian Job*. I think I was outside, pruning or some such. Easy-peasy just to slide the soldier back gently by its feet or that funny little plastic stand they all had, and that's just what Chris'd been about to do, he told me, when Rachel comes tripping down the stairs, sees what's what, rushes over and flicks it down the hole. He didn't get in a strop with her, he didn't cry. I've never known a child to cotton on so quick about satisfaction and how not to give it. But there it was, gone. I think that's what I did with that afternoon, as time passed, as another term went by and we sprinted and high-jumped and took our exams. Eased the soldier to halfway over the hole, looked at it and flicked it to its death. As for Alex, he didn't turn up for work half the time after Mum and Dad got back, maybe more than half, and Dad got narked and Mum got anxious and then he phoned with a tale about some family illness, all looking pretty bad, and vamoosed.

By the time I'd finished thinking it all through I found I'd gone past our house and was on the main road, nearly at my bus stop. That put the wind up me, not so much missing our house as remembering how I'd felt the night of the writers' meeting, after the drink with Trish, when I'd stepped off the bus and straight into whatever wanted to get me. No, not whatever, no point pussyfooting. Mr Patience. I didn't dash back to the house like I had that night but I took it pretty smartish. In the living room I saw the album exactly as I'd left it, only now I wouldn't have been surprised if the sticker under that photo from the Seven Stars had changed itself to *New Year's 1969, Dad and his apprentice, Alex Kinsella, tickle, tickle*. But I didn't look, I just took my cup through to the kitchen and chucked out the last of tea and washed it and turned it upside down on the drainer and stared at it.

That bit of fancy about the sticker turned my thoughts another way. Mrs Barton had brought the album round yesterday. I don't know the ins and outs of international post. Stuff from Georgie just arrives when it arrives, like mine to her, but let's say the album reached this country by Wednesday and then hung about a bit. Wednesday night was the writers' meeting, Wednesday night was the retro bloke at the side of the hall with his greyish shapeless effort and his face in the gloaming. Carnaby Alex come back from the mists in the hold of a plane. And Carnaby Alex having a savage go at my field and my church before I got to them that same night, gouging, blizzarding, tearing down the ivy, stripping off the leaves till there was just the one clump to hide that terrified little bird.

If anyone had told me a story like that before I'd have said God help us, you're proper gone out. But it made sense to me right then, staring down at the drainer, at the maker's doo-dad on the bottom of the cup. And it seemed to me that, though I could never have known it, he was part of why I'd found my world in the first place, my field and its butterfly snow and my old church with its wall and its trees, and why I'd needed to. And now he'd done for them and had taken about as long over it as he had over me with his hands and his grunting and his cable-rubber johnny. I was half way through thinking, well, at least he used one but I scotched that. I wasn't giving him everything.

Of a sudden there's his nibs in the kitchen. Just in? he asks and I realise I've still got my coat on. He starts on about his chat with the head coach, the new ground for their team, how the coach is all for it but he has his doubts now he knows which one it is, near the valley on the far side of town, low-level, possible flood-risk, and anyway he's sure he read somewhere that the conservation bods were bidding to have it zoned off to encourage this and that to come there, which would make sense since that stretch of valley's wild enough and without thinking I start to talk, so for a bit the kitchen's full of the cons about the new ground and the Seven Stars on New Year's Day 1969 and Alex's first couple of meals with us and how he hopped to it with the wash-up without being asked. And then his nibs stopped and let me talk how I hadn't meant to except I'd been through it all to myself round to the playing fields and past our house and nearly down to the bus stop where he'd been, sort of been, waiting on Wednesday night, Carnaby Alex, having skedaddled there after the writers' do had broken up and while Trish and me were raising our first glass in the bar, and since I'd been through it all to myself I just couldn't stuff it back into my mind unsaid or deep in my heart like some of those posh debs who get all deceived and horrified in my murder mysteries.

Why didn't you tell me all this before? He didn't say that, fair play to him. Instead he put the kettle on and then started to unbutton my coat with one hand and stroke my arm with the other till, bless him, he stepped back like he suddenly thought he was doing what he shouldn't and I started blinking, harder and harder the more my eyes stung, and I got hold of his hand and guided it back to the buttons still waiting. That made for a complete silence till I said about the hole round the heating pipe and Chris's game of soldiers, which he nodded at, and how Rachel had put the kibosh on it that one time, which he shook his head at, and how I'd copied her if he saw what I meant and done it pretty bloody well, too, till the album and the Seven Stars photo knocking the breath out of me like the front door had that afternoon. So I suppose I answered what he didn't ask.

When he'd got me settled with a tea at the kitchen table he went through to the hall. I heard him talking to the head coach, cancelling what was apparently meant as a surprise for me that evening, a meal with the coach and his wife at that pub they've just reopened near the farm shop, top chef, rave reviews. I got myself ready to start feeling bad but then realised I didn't have to, I'd done all that kind of feeling, that game was played out. It was nice, though, to hear him say how about next Saturday evening instead and it must have been all right because he said good good good in that quick way he has which used to get on Rachel's nerves and of course he'd add another 'good' each time she complained. Down goes the phone and I check to see if there's another tea in the pot for him but he doesn't come back and I'll bet he's looking at the album, that photo, and he starts his sort of breathy whistling which always means he'll be an age with whatever he's about.

So I go drifting, back to Rachel this time. Wondering if something like that ever happened to her and if that explains her rigmarole, get a bloke keen and treat him like dirt. If that's her way of dealing with it, though, it's too sad for words because, for one, it's like she's getting it all back in her head each time she gives a bloke the push and, for two, she's probably lost any number of good 'uns that way, especially if they were like the ones we met. *I hope some prime catch sweeps her off her feet,* said Georgie's note, *before she can open her mouth.* You know your niece a treat, Georgie. She can't not open it. I should really talk to Rachel. I'm not my mum though they say that's who daughters always turn into. But not me, not for this. Maybe if I mug up a bit on human-facing management and a few facts about West Hampstead, that'll get her off guard.

Then his nibs is in the kitchen doorway and Kinsella, you say? he asks and I nod and notice the time on the clock and make to get up, hoping I've remembered to defrost those drumsticks but he bends down and gets me back in the chair and tops up my tea and says how about a Chinese? which sounds lovely because the Golden Boat on the main road's just gone under new management and

166

it's a hundred times better than before. Good good good, he says and kisses the top of my head and I can feel my eyes come on to stinging even more and he kisses me again and finds the Boat's menu and puts it by my arm and tells me to take my time. Then he's off to the phone again and this time it sounds like he's calling one of his colleagues because it's pauses and then his hmm-hmm-hmm, like his good good good, so I can tell he's jotting stuff down.

And I realised something. Not once did I say to him I'd rather try to forget it now because not once did I say it to myself. It's like whatever the reverse of the law of diminishing returns is, which is another hot catchphrase with our kid of a manager when all he means is some this-week-only dodge from head office didn't work and their new dodge is double the rubbish, but of course he'd never actually say that because what head office comes up with is holy writ so the fault must lie in another quarter, which is another of his faves. Doubling, yes, let's call it that, the law of doubling returns. I know you'll never tell, said every finger of the hand on my face, every grunt, every push. But I told it clear through to myself on my walk, start to finish. I shook his hiding-place loose, you might say. And it fell to bits when I found myself telling his nibs. So I suppose what I'm saying is that, sitting there with the last of the tea, hearing his pauses and hmm-hmms, I proper astonished myself. I didn't want anything to diminish. Double away, I said to myself, and I raised my cup in a toast. And after that I made a lovely choice from the Boat menu, for him too, well, no choice as such there because I knew he'd say the usual,

167

and I walked through the living room and squeezed his shoulder where he was sat on the sofa with a note-pad and I went to phone in the order and I said, yes, half an hour will be fine, and then, almost without thinking, I phoned Trish.

A one-hour Poirot on the telly that evening and then, just in time, another channel for a full-length Morse. And we make the Chinese last nearly all of it, sitting side by side on the sofa, him squeezing me now and then, taking up my fork hand, which I'd usually get ratty about, say something about, oh yes, and who has to get the covers cleaned? But not this time and he even takes the containers to the kitchen once we're all done and I can hear him washing them out and that's love, laugh if you like. I don't push him about the call to his workmate and he doesn't say because he'll tell me in his own time and anyway this is simple and safe, right now, like Mrs Pooley's house, and I want it to stay as such. And that night he doesn't mutter or thrash about, he holds me like he used to in the days that turned out to be Rachel coming.

And it's breakfast all sorted next morning, eggs and toast at the ready when I come into the kitchen. As we're finishing up he starts rubbing the backs of his hands which always means he's about to get serious with either DIY or the laptop. So, Kinsella, he says and goes into the living-room and in a bit, sure enough, I can hear the tapping on the keys and those little wind-bell noises that tell you something's leading somewhere.

About half an hour later, after I'd done the wash up and got myself ready to face the world, he called me to come and sit with him at the living-room table. He had the laptop in front of him and the note-pad at his elbow with a list on it. Business sites, it turned out, Link-this-and-that, Find a Tradesman, most all of them crossed out except for one. He'd got them from his mate, he said, and, ok, he could have found them himself but the mate was more on the commercial insurance side and had them at his fingertips. As I got myself proper comfy he gave me a look that was sort of worried and chuffed together. Then he angled the laptop my way and I saw the name along the top of the screen, *Sunlight At Your Service*, the one he hadn't crossed off, and the site was about Port Sunlight, civic amenities in that part of the Wirral, tradesmen and what-have-you. The page he'd got to was a list of electricians in the area. And there he was between a Kinross and a Kinsey. Go on, says his nibs and pushes the mouse my way. So I clicked him.

Well, his nibs had already been through it himself because he pointed at this and that but mainly he just let me look. So, then. Mr Patience had scuttled back home, near enough, and done alright for himself too because Port Sunlight's on the posh side. Looked like he'd had his page done professionally or got a son to do it or a grandson because that's the joke these days, isn't it, how they're all born to it while the old 'uns look on all baffled. Logo very fancy, A and K intertwined with a plug rising up between them like the head of a snake, which said it all. Halfway down was a list of where he'd been for his trade and when, reverse order, and his nibs scrolled it slowly so it was like the credits at the end of a film. Just as well I wasn't drinking tea when he got to the bottom or I'd have splattered a mouthful all over everywhere. *1968-1969: Lead Technician, William Mostyn, Electrics and Mechanics, Biddulph, Staffordshire.* For a moment there I was madder than that afternoon had ever made me. Lead technician was bad enough but putting it before my dad's name and having the entry there at all, like my poor trusting dad was just a rung on his ladder, that was the old tin lid. I know, tradesfolk have to big themselves up, everyone does and the truth of such lists might be a case of more or less. I'd give anything to see what fairy-tales our kid of a manager smuggled in on his cv. Still and all.

I think that entry decided me. His nibs said nothing, then or after, but that was showing love again, daft though it sounds. He'd found him, he'd sort of brought him to me. Now, as you might say, the man was mine. Probably he'd had to do some scrabbling in his time, who didn't? but the screen said he'd done all right, maybe wasn't working at all or not much, because what would he be now, late sixties? easily that. Probably had chaps under him, son or sons, at any rate blokes who worked an honest day and didn't just clear off after they'd dealt with a kerfuffle in their trousers. You'd hope. No photo of him, thankfully, but an email and phone and house address. Playford Way. Come out to play. Dear Prudence.

Power. That's what I felt out of nowhere. Never in all this world did I think I'd feel it about that afternoon. And his nibs not saying a word, just putting it in front of me like a box of chocolates with the lid off, that made it all the stronger. No, not power, that's a bloke's word. So's control. Let's say possibilities, possibilities at my fingers' ends, arranged like that, no, arrayed, that'd give poeting Trish a run for her money. Because the story isn't meant to end like this, is it? It's meant to end with oh, all a long time ago and it was different back then and bit late to be dredging it up, look at the age of you, and anyway, your word against his. Which he might say, probably would, in his older voice, maybe full of years of beer and fags, if I phoned him, or with lots of exclamation marks and dot-dot-dots if I emailed him, or with eyes like razors and a good showing of his tribe round him, wife included, on the door-step at Playford Way. Or maybe not wife included, maybe he's a widower or divorced two, three times over. A maintenance-man. Or just, I never did, it didn't happen, you know you, you're a liar, missus, money is it? You don't want to come it with me. Prick-tease to end them all, you were.

But all that, it doesn't matter. In one of those Easter poems I dip into, the devotional ones, the quill-merchant efforts, there's the line, 'I see you as you stand.' That's where it all comes from, they come from, the possibilities, the tingle at the ends of my fingers as you might say. I see him as he stands and he hasn't a clue I see him, he's bat-blind. I could be walking up behind him, he wouldn't know. I could be stepping in front of him in a park. I could be pushing open his front door when someone forgot to close it, one of the grandkids, someone the age I was when it was the Mac Fisheries bag and Mrs Pooley saying PT. Yes. I can choose my time, tomorrow, next week, you name it, to lift the phone or get his nibs to crank up the laptop or shake the travel-rug and check the mileage from here to there. Or all of same.

171

Choice and possibilities. I should write that on a scrap of paper, shove it under our kid of a manager's nose and say, there you are, Sonny-Jim, this month's slogan, I've worked out my commission. And the smile his nibs gave me when he closed the laptop, it said I know, I see you see him. Person of interest located, as Morse's Lewis might say. Whatever you want. Whenever you like. Nothing, everything.

Come lunchtime he says, never mind waiting for next Saturday, how about giving that refurbished pub a dry run now? Trish phoned back as we were getting our coats on. She'd already got hold of the motherly sort, who was delighted and said of course, of course I could read at the next meeting, a couple of folk would be away so no problem with a slot.

Any time now Georgie will email his nibs or phone when it's midnight there and cockcrow here and ask. Did it get there safely? What did I think? All our yesterdays, eh? Famn damilies, as Richie would say. I'll have to look through it to the end. When I feel able. Or maybe she'll write, she's one of the few who still go for letters. That'll be better. Give me time to work out what I want to say. Because, I mean, after telling myself all through on that walk, and telling his nibs, it's only right that she should know, certainly before that other one does, with his Carnaby years long gone, jabbing his finger into my face on the doorstep at Playford Way. His old finger now, maybe his arthritic finger, good for not much except, as you might say, tickling the air. But I wouldn't want Georgie to feel bad, to feel like she'd stirred things up by sending the album. Awoken them. Thanks, Trish. So I'll

172

be careful. In fact I might not say a dicky bird to her yet. There'll be time to say it in the best way it could be said. Choice again. Possibilities.

The refurbished pub's lovely. Tasty savoury biscuits for afters and it turns out they sell them, they sell all sorts, some deal with the farm shop, so I got a packet to take over to Trish's next Friday night. I'll have to see what wine our kid of a manager's pushing at the moment, too, and if it's anything less than that Vasse I'll diminish his returns.

Speaking of Trish, when she phoned back she was full of oh, Helen, let me hear it next Friday night, what you're going to read. A dialogue of trespass, I nearly said, but to be honest I don't know what it might be. I might not even have anything for Friday night. I'll need to take my time. It won't be the whole kit and caboodle, obviously. But maybe something that says without saying, which seems to be what gets a lot of writers in a holy fizz. Elliptical intimations, to pinch his nibs' phrase. I know I said I didn't want to write my world down. But maybe, how things are, it could be a way to get it back. Or start to. So something about a field with deep gouges but where snow-butterflies are already dipping about, against the time the ground levels itself up. Or a churchyard with one streak of ivy already on the wall and leaves enough on the trees, and birds enough among all of them.

The End

Mister Sixth

The triangle of light shimmered on the wall, stilled, shimmered again. At the third shimmer Evan got out of bed. There was a gap at the top where the curtains met. He hadn't noticed before. Well, he'd had the reading lamp on and everything goes pitch-black when you turn a light off. He wouldn't have noticed at all if he hadn't remembered the transom window. Carefully arranging the curtains, he returned to bed, only to remember that he'd forgotten the transom again. Getting up a second time, he slid a hand gingerly behind the curtains so as not to disturb the folds. The transom was shut. Part of him knew it would be but another part, the part that liked to get him up and about in the dead of night, had whispered that perhaps he hadn't made sure. Evan had been making sure about all sorts for years, then suffering the whispers, then making sure again. His ex-wife had more than once wondered if, in a previous life, he'd been a burglar who suddenly got lonely in the middle of a job and just had to say hello.

All the checking and whispering were perhaps justified now, or at least as far as they could ever be. It wasn't his bedroom. It was Hugh's. Or rather, it had been Hugh's when Hugh was a child, a schoolboy, an undergraduate, which was when he and Evan had met. But Hugh was married now and he and his wife were sleeping across the landing in what was his parents' room, and they'd temporarily moved into what his mother still called the new extension, although that had been added one summer an age ago when Evan had been visiting, when he and Hugh were still alternately studious and carefree and, for a while, he hadn't felt compelled to check so much. Evan had wondered at the need for the extension. Compared to his childhood home, Hugh's was baronial, a Victorian detached, ivy and trellises and gravel that swept, yes, swept, round in front of the steps up to the front door. Evan had never seen gravel sweeping before. He thought it only did that in novels or TV series where chauffeur after chauffeur pulled car after car up in front of seriously-panelled front doors and waited while elegant people, laughing, arguing or just tight-lipped, spilled out for a weekend party or the reading of a will. He'd often wondered what it would be like to be such people. No fussing over transoms for them. If they spotted a triangle of light on a night wall they'd summon a uniformed figure who would cough discreetly and extinguish it. As for where the light came from, he certainly wasn't going to investigate that. Anyway, it was high summer. Hardly a coal-hole sky.

There were other folk dotted about the sleeping house besides Hugh's family. There were Evan and Hugh's university friends and their spouses. No children, though: they would have been farmed out. This wasn't a time for children. It was a milestone reunion, a time to look back, even recapture something or other or at least watch its ghost flickering on the walls like that light.

Lying in the dark, Evan took in the vague shapes of the room. They seemed like the outlines of roofs and chimneys you'd see on a backdrop to a stage. He wouldn't have been surprised to see an aerial popping up here, the silhouette of a cat slinking past there, perhaps

175

hunting for a transom that was open. Since Hugh's departure for the grown-up life, the room had obviously been designated for lumber. Storage boxes rose against a far wall, more lamps than any one space could use sat on more shelves than anyone but a bookworm would need. It was all very tidy and the room had the space to take it. Still, lying there, Evan felt like he'd been employed by someone with a frivolous notion of a nightwatchman's duties: start Monday, bring own pyjamas. He wondered what was in the boxes and on the shelves. He hadn't looked much at the latter. Well, it had been a late night, everyone just arrived, greeted by Hugh and his wife and his parents, his sister and her husband, his other sister and someone she insisted was not her husband, she didn't go in for that antique carry-on—all making up a composite host. But Hugh, of course, was the true master of ceremonies. As he had uncharacteristically phrased it in the email to Evan and their friends, it was a big gig. *Twenty-five years since we got kicked out of the ivied halls and into the big bad world. I just had to gather you all up.*

Evan stared at where the triangle of light had been. The world had hardly been bad to Hugh. His firm's client list boasted some big and lucratively litigious names. Their university friends, too, those summoned to the milestone, had made out very nicely. So had Evan himself…perhaps…if you looked at his progress from a certain angle. From another angle it seemed that he was still ducking and diving in a way that was a bit odd for someone now in their forties. Adult evening classes, short-term uni contracts, the occasional, very occasional, summer junket, holding forth on Keats and Shelley in

176

Rome, Joyce in Paris. Well, not odd. Rather, not serious, which was the phrase he'd seen staring back at him that evening from the eyes of Hugh's parents, his sisters, and yes, Hugh himself in the split-second before he blinked it away. Old Evan, Hugh had always called him and his family had picked up on it. This was fine when he and Hugh were students and for the earlier milestone shindigs: twenty-fifth birthdays, five years out of uni, thirtieth birthdays, ten years out of uni, the weddings, the christenings. Now, though, the rest of the reunion crew had started calling him Old Evan too, and it was beginning to grate. There was a whiff of disdain about it, as though it trailed *what is he like?* in its wake. No one else in the group was Old anything.

It was a familiar dodge, Evan told himself, surprised that he hadn't truly got it till now. Always have someone in your orbit for purposes of compare and contrast. Even when things were bad, when your fellow executives were mutinous, when your constituency majority might be halved, when some off-his-face-on-fairy-dust celebrity was threatening to take his legal business elsewhere, you could say, well, at least I'm not Old Evan. Sighing in the darkness, Evan told himself he was being too harsh, too sensitive. It didn't work.

A prodigious memory, Hugh had. Well, no, probably a constantly updated address book and a super-efficient secretary. He'd kept in serious touch with everyone from their uni crowd. At times he'd probably told X that he was getting married or Y that she was expecting before they knew themselves. And over the years, everyone had gathered for everything as though compelled by sorcery.

177

Or by a need to park, if only briefly, what life had become. Well, nearly everyone. Geoff Porter had turned up just once, for someone's twenty-fifth. Geoff, whose Blackburn accent was his Old Evan tag. Big, uncomfortable in purpose-bought casual wear, he'd been cornered by one of Hugh's sisters who said she was really hoping to really take in the Pennines one day, making them sound as distant as Tibet. 'Stuff this,' he'd muttered to Evan as he left early, claiming the need to be in Glasgow next day for a christening. 'I wasn't their bloody ape then and I'm not now.' However he'd done it, he'd ever after managed to evade Hugh's tentacles. Glasgow might have been true but the last Evan had known was a postcard from Greece. 'On my second taverna,' it said. 'Negotiations nearly done.' A publican, Geoff's dad had been. In the genes. Evan had said nothing to Hugh. Geoff wouldn't have thanked him for waking up one morning to find his second taverna filled with expensive luggage and Hugh clapping him on the back with 'Ecky-thump, our Geoff, you've proper got on.'

A thin line of light appeared where the triangle had been. The mystique of fabric, thought Evan. As he'd been lying there pondering, the curtains had worked themselves apart like inchworms taking their leave. They'd done that in his bedroom when he was a kid. Then, as now, the windows had been closed, the curtains had been checked, checked again. Well, he wasn't getting up now. Some things you couldn't explain. And he realised that this included Hugh's motives for all these reunions. It wasn't as if he didn't see the crew in ones and twos between the milestones. He and Evan had met up enough times over the years, though recently this had dwindled. Recently, in fact, Hugh had started postponing, pleading any number of plausible things: flights to deal with suddenly shaky contracts, rescheduled palavers with this or that QC. To start with they'd rearranged but last time Hugh hadn't come back to him with alternative dates and all of a sudden, weeks later, he realised he hadn't offered any either.

But come on, Evan told himself in the dark, Hugh had been there for him when he and Pennie had split up. The dark waited for him to warm to this saving theme but the theme just quivered a moment like the thin line of light on the wall, which was now a bit thicker, and then vanished. Hugh had been there-ish, nothing more. Perhaps his concern had been genuine. It was just that, both times they met for a heart-to-heart, his demeanour quickly became, well, professional, to the point where Evan expected him to declare, with a hand-masked cough, his hourly fee. Thinking about it afterwards, he wondered whether Hugh was honing his working manner on the situation, a murmur here, an emphasis there. And perhaps Hugh knew he was and wanted to back-pedal, which was why, not long after the second heart-to-heart, he invited Evan down to his parents' place for the weekend. He'd be there with his wife, Tarah-with-an-h-for-some-reason, and of course the toddlers, but everyone would love to see him. But it turned out that others from the uni crew were there as well, and their wives with or without h's, their husbands whose polysyllabic names were pronounced in a gulp. Despite the bonhomie, the shows of solicitude, it was

179

really another milestone do and Evan was the date in the diary. Evan, eh? Back on the bench. Ready meals for one. D'you think we should introduce him to…or have him along when we…don't you think…or don't you? Old Evan. What is he like?

The line of light on the wall quivered again. Squinting, Evan willed it to disappear. It wouldn't budge. He closed his eyes. Why did Hugh insist on planting these milestones? And why still here? His own house was plenty big enough and apparently he had his eye on something bigger. Well, this was where they'd all started. Tradition. Continuity. Was that it for Hugh, was that all? Where was friendship? Alive and kicking on all those well-tended faces or just an echo out of twenty-odd years ago? And why did he himself keep coming back? Habit? Auld Lang Syne? The hope that, this time, something would be there, some atmosphere, even some moment, that he'd been looking for, something Hugh had, or one of them had, that would finally yield itself up and season his life for the good? He wrinkled his face round a silent laugh. What a bunch of somethings. For a moment he imagined himself with legs stretched out under a sun-drenched awning. A drink of unfamiliar colour was placed before him. 'Have you not tried it before?' asked Geoff Porter. 'It's good, is that.'

But sleep was the thing now. Full day tomorrow. The banquet that was breakfast, then a good walk ('Stride out, man,' Hugh's father had barked once, looking back to see Evan loafing about in the rear), then one of Hugh's mother's elaborate picnics ('Oh dear, Evan, do you need another napkin?'), then a swing round to the village

180

cricket ground where Hugh and a polysyllable were scheduled to go first in for a scratch visitors' side. One of Hugh's sisters and Tarah had got up an entertainment for after supper; the words 'with participation' had risen desolatingly upon the air that very evening.

It was all a right job of work...speaking of which, he'd have to get onto that American College outside Woodstock again. Summer was a-wasting and he'd had no word about that lecturing for the first semester. If they did want him, he'd have to do some juggling with his Open University work, maybe push for Arts Foundation groups in Gloucester or Cheltenham so as to keep everything in one broad area. Almost everything. The third-year Literature course he could do nothing about. It was Wolverhampton and that was that. Still, he'd travelled further than all that before, watched more roads unspool, made shift with dodgy taps in more Travelodges than he'd probably need this time. Manchester and King's Lynn had dictated his axis one year and he'd moved smartly enough between them. The memory of that triumph, even with its flat tyres and stopped trains, ushered sleepiness in. He was just murmuring goodnight to the light on the wall when something made him open his eyes. Hugh's face was inches from his own.

Evan scrunched up his eyes and counted to ten, then forced one open. Relaxing, he opened the other. There was no Hugh. Yet there was. Between Evan and the light on the wall stood an image as sharp as the real thing had been twenty-five years ago. Again Hugh looked angry, contemptuous, about to collar someone and sort this bloody nonsense out. Again he spoke those words. Evan had let the memory bury itself long ago. Now it had risen again among the milestones.

It was a daft thing, almost nothing at all. In late autumn of their final year, Hugh had shoved a leaflet at him. *Tales and Tellers Digest,* it said, with details of a three-day event up at the University of Sheffield the following April. Submissions were invited of tales, no more than fifteen minutes long, on a subject of the writer's choosing (with the usual caveats—no defamation of living characters, nothing wildly experimental, no porn). Twenty-five of these would be shortlisted. On the Friday and Saturday, the lucky twenty-five would read their tales, at the end of which ten would get even luckier and go forward to a read-off on the Sunday: their tales again plus a ten-minute portrait of someone living or dead, famous or obscure. After that, those final ten would be ranked and called back up to be glad-handed by the judges. All would get some memento but the top three would get a year's subscription to *Tales and Tellers Digest,* the top two would also get a specially-inscribed 'Teller's Pen' and the overall victor—'Spinner of the Year', as the leaflet had it—would also get a book on how to research, shape and declaim the right tale for every conceivable occasion. Evan had said it all looked seriously strange so, yes, he was up for it.

That wasn't Hugh's take. He saw it as practice for future glory, a chance to play with and thus more deeply understand the rigours of a tort or contract brief. Soon, after serious plunges into case-histories, his offering was in the bag. Joseph Marklew from Lower Gornal, Dudley, a chargehand at Brightson's Rolling Mills, was hanged in March 1922 for the murder of Rebekah Devlin, a widow, and her daughters, Florence (10) and Bea (7), of 9 Cadeby Street, Princes End, Tipton. He hadn't known them nor they him. He just traced the surname and did it. At his trial it emerged that his sole animus towards them stemmed from an incident ten years before, when, as a soldier in Ireland, he'd been attacked by a Pad Devlin in the grounds of Kilmallock Priory, down below the Barracks. As Hugh said, the old grudge had gone underground and might never have surfaced. Who knew what accident of circumstance had dragged it free? A perennial headache for lawyers, that—the play of reasonless compulsion which the law could never quite contain. Yet still you had to decide, to judge, otherwise where was security, where was order? Fascinating, Hugh said.

Evan's choice was John Cartwright, a boy at his secondary school. John's older brother had a menagerie of foreign snakes and spiders, some illegal, which would have given Hugh the willies. After a monster row with his brother, John had freed a diamondback rattlesnake, which gloried in its terrifying freedom for a good two days before the Fire Service and the RSPCA ran it to ground in the foliage of nearby Eccleshall Park, surrounded by bits and ends of squirrels which hadn't been to its liking. Evan told it straight but emphasised the contrast between exotica, particularly this specimen's hark-back to New Mexico and Baja California, and the walls and privets and cut-throughs by which his own early years were hemmed in.

As for the pen-portraits required for Sunday's finals, Hugh's was a briskly confident tour round Bartholomew Gosnold, Elizabethan lawyer and leading light in the colonising of Virginia. Evan's was a rather baggy reminiscence of Bill Hallmark, one of two brothers who ran a local allsorts shop and who hired himself out as a pigeon-whisperer among the local fanciers. Evan wasn't that bothered about either of his pieces but, well, he'd never been to Sheffield and his sister was a big fan of Joe Cocker, one of its famous sons. Just the job, a weekend away.

He and Hugh heard back from the organisers. They'd made it into the hopeful twenty-five. Hugh looked Marklew and Gosnold over again and again. Evan let John Cartwright and Bill Hallmark be. The following April, they checked into their Sheffield b&b on the Thursday night and, next morning, marvelled at the array of tale-tellers—hirsute and shaven-headed, leathered and gowned—around them at the meet-and-greet. There followed tales of courage and foolery, dreams and pratfalls, excursions into the lives of Hereward the Wake, Pocahontas, Queen-Victoria's bobbin-keeper, Aunt Mavis and her budgie which could sing 'La Mer', the pilot in the Buddy Holly plane crash. And at the end of the Saturday, Evan's rattlesnake came eighth and Hugh's murderous chargehand a narrow-miss twelfth. After the announcement and while the MC—a fizzy American who smuggled 'enjoy' into every sentence—was inviting everyone back to next day's big read-off, Hugh began shifting about in his chair and muttering that he might as well clear off, but not to worry, he wouldn't ask Evan to compensate him, even in part, for the b&b room he wouldn't be using that night. Hugh had a way of jumping up straight-limbed like someone who saw musical chairs as a variant of drill parade. He did so then but not before he'd stared as deeply into Evan's eyes as that ambushing image had in the darkened room and said, 'That should have been me, Evan.' Then he was gone. 'Wow, something left on the stove?' the MC asked of his speeding back. Only the buffeting of swing doors replied.

Lying stock-still, Evan let the rest of that weekend spool out. On the Sunday, his reminiscence of the pigeon-whisperer did him enough of a favour to shift him up to sixth overall. He got what his maternal grandmother would have called a sustificate and details of the Tale Tellers' International Convention that summer in Lille, including the sop that, as one of the top ten this time, he could submit two tales for the price of just over one. Later, he got good-humoured dealing from Geoff Porter, who, for at least a week, would announce his approach with 'It's the Evanator! The sixth most famous bod in the universe!' Evan had only told Hugh, who seemed to want to know as a way of tidying up the whole business. But Hugh told everyone. Whether or not he repeated his own sour judgment, Evan never knew. After Geoff's last chuckle died down, Sheffield was never mentioned again.

The line of light on the wall was fading. Here and there, the lumber was defining itself, showing bits of colour. What time is it? thought Evan but didn't check. Sheffield hadn't been mentioned again yet perhaps it had

185

and still was. Every reunion was Hugh's way of saying 'This is me, Old Evan, and it certainly isn't you.' And to cap it all, here he was in Hugh's old room, his single bed, like the tagalong cousin who has to be put somewhere. Again he tried telling himself he was being too sensitive—come on, water under the bridge, one of his own nephews was nearly as old as the time-lapse since Sheffield happened. But Hugh was the man with the address-book, the birthday list, the mind like pincers. By now he probably didn't need to consult details when preparing yet again to issue a milestone summons. He simply remembered, hoarded. Come to think of it, he'd potted Bartholomew Gosnold's dizzying life with barely a note to hand.

Slowly the room brightened. Evan found himself staring at the bookshelves opposite the bed. Even now he could make out Hugh's name on the spines of important-looking notebooks in their neat piles. For a few minutes he imagined Geoff's taverna again, and his other taverna, again heard him pronounce some refreshment right good. Then he looked at his watch.

Half an hour later his case was in his car and he was filling his travel flask with coffee from the breakfast sideboard. Lovely coffee, Hugh's mother made, he'd give her that. But she didn't seem to be about. Nobody was. He'd concocted something. The American College had left a text message asking him back for a second interview, this time for a full lectureship. So sorry but he'd need to head home and prepare. But he let all that go. It was cowardly. Something crossing his mind, he crept upstairs. The door across the landing was ajar. He heard Hugh's wife sigh and quietly cough. There were no male sounds, not even a snore. Hugh was up and about, too, it seemed.

Evan waited by his car, unheeding the curtains opening above him, the face or two looking out. But no footsteps cracked on twigs or crunched the gravel. After about fifteen minutes he emptied his mind, got in and swung round, taking the driveway slowly in case Gosnold's advocate should appear. Nothing, except that he had to pull over to let the post-van by. Accelerating along the road, he remembered that Geoff Porter's cousin had taken over the Blackburn pub. He still had that address. His mind settled round a late summer holiday on…Kos, was it? Cephalonia? He imagined Geoff and himself in the cool of the evening, clinking glasses, Geoff punching his shoulder playfully: 'The Evanator. Remember? Mister Sixth, eh? Hope you wrote some more.' He hadn't.

The nearby village welcomed him with white picket fences on either verge and asked him to drive carefully. He tightened and loosened his grip on the wheel. He wouldn't be surprised if Hugh had been about all the time, had seen him stow his case, observed from a corner as he filched the coffee. Maybe it was a refinement of 'This is me, Old Evan, and it certainly isn't you.' Invite and invite until that one reunion too many. The one that forced the rattlesnake memoirist into final retreat. And of course they must have watched and planned, too, Joseph Marklew, Bartholomew Gosnold, which was why Hugh had been drawn to them. Probably. Old Marklew. Old Gosnold.

187

Just as Evan passed the first sign for the motorway, Hugh came back from his morning jog and saw the space among the cars. He turned full circle, scratched his head. Footsteps sounded behind him and the man who wasn't his other sister's husband, never mind that antique carry-on, told him he'd seen the divorced chappie hanging about and then driving off. Food's piping hot, he added, and went back in.

But Hugh, arms folded, walked slowly down the drive and back, ending up again where Evan's car wasn't. He frowned. He shook his head. His arms dropped to his sides. He had to be called in to breakfast, twice.

Never Any Sometimes

'Dad, we'll be late.'

Phil Holmwood came to the head of the stairs and looked down at his middle daughter. He saw her place one hand on her hip and clutch the top of the banister post with the other. It looked as though she'd been rehearsing various attitudes of reproach and, just too late, chosen that.

'I'm nearly ready,' he said, not adding, 'For what?'

It had been quite straightforward. He'd drive to Birmingham International for the Euston train. Having heard nothing, he'd assumed that his wife's Eurostar had got in on time and the connection was fine. An hour before leaving, though, he saw a figure loom at the front door, one that the patterned glass could not break up. Rebecca. She'd blown in already speaking. No Eurostar for Mum. No faffing at Euston. Pam's visit to an old friend in Normandy, Phil learned, had been one big surprise. Already there were a couple she and the friend had known while studying: a varsity romance, marriage in the second year. She'd lost touch with them but the friend hadn't. And apart from that, said Rebecca (her all-weather phrase), the couple were returning on the same day as Mum. So…Eurostar forgotten, online search, Pam booked on their flight to Manchester, their car waiting, a swift call to Buffery Manor just outside Alcester where they were staying on their way back to Swanage, a room for Pam, table for seven that evening— and apart from that, Pam heading off with them tomorrow morning, their special guest at Swanage for, ooh, however long she liked.

'What about Gilly?' Phil had asked, glad of a banister post himself by that point. 'Are we meant—?'

'Nelly Dean's seeing to her.' The relish with which Rebecca abused the name of her older sister Gwendolen was, like her catch-phrase, undimmed.

'Dad, come on,' she called up now and Phil, descending the stairs, wondering if he looked all right but knowing he'd soon be told if not, thought glumly of that programme which, in original circumstances, he'd have been back for. 'We're not having one of those Smart TVs', sounded Pam in his head. 'Any of those catch-up thingies and you'd be living in it.'

'Is your tie supposed to look like that?' Phil shifted uncomfortably under his daughter's fashionista gaze. Mercifully, she didn't comment on anything else. They hardly spoke on the way to Alcester. She'd delivered the news and, from long experience, Phil knew that his part was as some nameless lord in Shakespeare: a nod, a hmm, a 'Say you so?'

Retirement: his pending—just part-time now—Pam's early and glorious. Always off, she was. The friends she had. The new friends she made. Arrangements changed on the hoof. Sometimes their annual holiday was grafted awkwardly onto her jaunts, usually meaning that he had to come back on his own. This Swanage thing wasn't unusual: believable but with a ring of desperate invention, as of a rookie playwright trying to finish Act Three with an hour before curtain up. He'd once assumed that, once he was done working, she'd invite him to join her on the wing. Now he suspected she wouldn't. He'd have to go mad-capping on his own, bumping into her, so to speak, only for the occasional long-calendared holiday. 'The garden needs sorting,' Pam had said more than once. 'Not to mention the attic.' Thus was the last phase of his strutting and fretting defined. Or not, he thought as they neared Alcester. He had nothing in mind and for sure he wasn't one of nature's madcaps. Still...

Far too bright. Several times Phil looked up at the faux-chandelier above the table and was mightily glad when the restaurant was dimmed just before their starters came.

Caroline and Jim. And James. From the start of the evening, from the handshakes and mwah-mwahs and drinks in the bar, he'd quietly scrupled to add 'it's James' when anyone became as informal as the occasion seemed to merit. Phil felt as though, rather than actually eating his dinner, he was being interviewed on his fitness for same. James had been a financial advisor on the south coast, capricious stocks and that. Something in the suburbs, thought Phil. Their garden was attended to by a local treasure. Their attic was James' den in the sky. Swanage, thought Phil. He'd heard jokes about it. No doubt there was a young lady from there.

But the wife said 'Just Carol's fine' and asked everyone all about themselves in a way that was jolly rather than intrusive. Court clerk had been her line. The tales she could tell—and did, a few, in a way that nicely balanced openness with the time-honoured disclaimer at the start of novels: any resemblance, living or dead, quite coincidental. Phil liked her. He wondered if he'd met them before, way back, but there'd been no chance to check with Pam and neither she nor they mentioned it, Carol because she was happy to be in the moment, James because he was James.

Phil looked across the table at his eldest, quietly smiling, showing interest in all she heard. Gwendolen's birth had soon put paid to any hankering he'd had for a son. From an early age she'd been his...no, not ally...more his rapporteur in the world of children. Yes, at times she'd grizzled as a girl, rolled eyes as a teenager. Underneath, however, there'd been wisdom, forbearance, especially where her mother was concerned. She'd take some unjustified telling in a way that somehow left Pam on the wrong foot, illustrated Wilde's dictum that you should forgive your enemies as nothing annoyed them so much. She must have done some fancy dancing, Phil thought, to get there this evening with Gilly. Perhaps she'd have a late-nighter afterwards on the laptop: a primary school didn't run itself. Perhaps her Rob had been due to go out but was suddenly in charge of their two. He wouldn't have demurred. As soon as they'd met him, as soon as he'd said his first charming words to Pam, Phil knew that here was another polite wrong-footer.

'Are you okay there, love?' said Carol, leaning to the head of the table, and Gilly smiled and said yes. They were better about all that these days, thought Phil, hotels and such. Plenty of clearance between them and the adjacent tables and hardly anyone gave the wheelchair a second look. A stunner, their youngest had been, which, looking back, was probably the only thing that drew that clown to her. Vanished clown now, thankfully. Motor-mouth Alex. Big talk, bright horizons, but underneath, well, Andy Capp was quite outclassed. After Gilly's accident, though, the cat got his tongue. 'I've tried to love her,' he'd insisted, barging into the house that morning, getting in first before the rumblings of divorce. 'I've done all I can…it's so not easy…she can't help it, I know and…but I'll always love her.'

'Wonder if she could have helped it,' Pam had murmured sometime later. 'Five goes it took her, the test. I mean, Philip, was she really watching the road?' He'd exploded at her as he'd never done before or since. Perhaps, he wondered now, she lived life on the wing because she was never quite sure that it wouldn't happen again. People you met hither and yon, winging like you, they were safe. Mild disagreements over the wine-list: that was probably as fractious as it got. But Gilly was doing just fine, a respected copy-editor, nicely settled in her adapted house, paying her way, going on holidays but sweetly steering the talk elsewhere if Phil suggested she might like one with Mum and Dad. 'He's a catch, that Alex,' Pam had said, often. Like her big sister, Gilly knew her mother.

'But apart from that we were late as it was so there was nothing I could do about his tie.' Rebecca had a special gurgle to go with her boom-boom remarks. It sort of spilled out of the final word—as now, when Phil found all eyes upon him.

'One of my clients,' said James, 'was just the same.

193

Chain-store chappie, sports and leisure. Fairish taste but could never match the tie. One had South Sea girlies all over it.'

'You must have had a good look,' said Gwendolen, at which Carol laughed, James didn't and Pam said "Scuse me, Gwendolen' in a chill rush. She'd never called her Gwen. Gilly gave her father a smile, almost nothing but warmer than Pam's at her Christmas best. Rebecca, determined that the topic should remain her party, reached over and tugged Phil's tie: 'Silly old bit of rag, eh, Dad?' she said in a brittle voice.

'No more need of 'em once you've hung up the working boots,' Carol twinkled, laying a hand on his arm. 'You'll have a ball, promise.'

'Will he?' The table fell silent. Everyone watched Pam as she drew herself up. 'Will he now?' She turned to Phil. 'A ball with the garden and the attic, my lad, and all your old tat to dispatch. That'll see you out and then some.'

'Mum.' Gilly edged herself forward in her chair.

Pam stared into her eyes as if attempting hypnosis: 'And when does he ever visit you, my lady? Hey?'

'Mum, he sometimes—'

'There was never any sometimes when I was on at him. Take her out, I said, get her comfortable behind the wheel, smooth the way for the lessons.'

'He offered, Mum. I was the one who—'

'Well if he'd ignored you and gone ahead and done it then maybe...and maybe you and Alex—'

'Mum.' Gwendolen now, quiet, firm, the head teacher curbing a loose-limbed child.

'Shush, you, Nelly Dean,' Rebecca hissed at her. 'You

and your granny name.'

'Rebecca that's enough.' Suddenly all eyes were back on Phil and he was in shock. Out of nowhere he'd sounded as he had when working up to that explosion at Pam. Gilly eased back slowly in her chair and stared at a point beyond the table. But there was no further need for shushing. Whatever it was, the enormity of what Pam was about to say overtook her. She sank back, confusion in her eyes. What had she been at? Showing real grief at last? Confessing the toll of a bottle of wine? Courting another explosion to underscore how the coming years would play out, two paths, his 'n' hers, east and west? Any or all, Phil thought. After another silence, during which James harried a mushroom round his plate, he asked Carol if Swanage was still a tourist pull.

'Can't move for them,' she said. 'Have to fight my way to the front door. Not.' She and he laughed together. Gwendolen mentioned a holiday there when she and Rob were first going out. The evening steadied itself.

Another surprise: the Buffery had a cancellation: 'I've brought some things on the off-chance,' said Rebecca; then, parrying the offer of a lift next day, 'I'll train it. Pick up my car from—' She indicated Phil with a twist of the thumb.

Bonhomie was mustered for the goodbyes. Phil waited in the car park, waved to Gwendolen and Gilly, then set off. Hanbury, Droitwich, the Worcester road. However it looked, he thought, he hadn't come up smelling like a rose so he shouldn't think it. Anything for a quiet life was all very well but the interest on it could sting your eyes. Had he pushed Pam away and not cared? Rebecca too? Did Gwen and Gilly love him in spite of himself? He considered his upcoming freedom and Carol's twinkle: 'You'll have a ball, promise.' As he turned for the Worcester road he saw himself online, checking suitable hotels, booking rooms for two. This time he wouldn't fade away. This time he'd insist. And he pictured Gilly's almost-nothing smile.

'Sing Ho! Stout Cortez'

Dave Frankiewicz descends the steps to the jetty and looks around as he's done several times since leaving the main street of Glengariff. Someone is bound to come after him to ask if he's looking for a boat across to Garinish Island and tell him that there probably won't be one. 'It's not worth it,' he imagines hearing, 'if it's just for yourself, like.'

And it doesn't look as though there'll be any other takers. It isn't the season for boat trips, it isn't the day. Everyone will be indoors with plenty of drink to hand and a warm anticipation of the New Year. Anyway, he doesn't want to cross to Garinish. Down between the two small launches, gently bobbing, will be fine. At the jetty's end he looks round one more time. Vaguely he notes that one boat is *The Queen of* something and the other is something *Jewel.* He places his rucksack on the ground and gingerly retrieves the urn. Unscrewing it, also gingerly, he pours its contents into the water between the boats.

'Sing Ho! Stout Cortez,' he whispers. 'Sing Ho, Pete.'

Forty years earlier, on a New Year's Eve as raw as this one, Dave finished smashing up a toilet and laid his lump-hammer aside before saying, 'You're a proper case.'

The figure he addressed was a head taller than he was and lanky with it. Dave's words didn't arrest the man's actions and he carried on making short work of a footbath and adding to the mounds of sundered porcelain between them. Only when he'd finished did he pause and say, as he'd said several times throughout the afternoon, 'I'm telling you. Special occasion means a special effort.'

And the occasion was special. Tomorrow would be the first time that the people of England had New Year's Day off. To celebrate, most of the employees at Timperley Builders and Plumbers, Suppliers to the Trade, were heading for the Arden Park Hotel just outside Wolverhampton. There would be a meal and drinks followed by dancing but before the dancing there would be a speech from the Gaffer and a few turns. The lanky figure had been working up something for that. The very thought of it had kept him warm for weeks since he hatched it and certainly through that raw afternoon while he and Dave, on orders from above, had been out in the far yard smashing up bathroom and kitchen fitments which, classed as seconds, were unfit for the salesroom.

'Look, Pete, you might get laughed out of town,' said Dave, steadying a sink-pillar between his legs. His tone wasn't unkind.

'Pete? Pete?'

'God help us,' muttered Dave as he induced a pair of deep cracks in the pillar. 'All right, then…Ronan O'Malley.'

They worked on.

Pete Hughes had long regarded his name as sad and unheroic. Everyone used it. What else would they call him? Still it galled him and the official flourish that turned it into *Hughes, P* on pay packets and delivery sheets did nothing to redeem it. Pete was a child of fancy.

198

It had sustained him from his early years in Glengariff, County Cork, and had come to his rescue mightily when his father, of an itinerant turn of mind, had uprooted his family to the Black Country. Once there, however, he hadn't found anything to his taste in the plentiful work of the time so he'd drunk himself to a standstill and thence the grave, leaving his family to make shift as best they could.

Pete could only remember two things about him: an excitable right fist and his claim, urged when he was in his cups, to be descended from Grace O'Malley, Elizabethan Queen of Connacht. This had cut no ice with Pete's mother: 'Descent is right,' she retorted once. 'They're looking for foundry-men at Stewarts and Lloyds but ye won't descend into that, errah ye won't. I'd wish for your Queenie to canter up and hoosh your erse into it.'

But Pete was caught. His mother's contempt was of a piece with the attitude that he himself endured from peers, teachers, everyone who refused to give themselves up to imagining. Something began to sing in his blood. He saw himself as different, the victim of a jest of fortune, like one of those blue-bloods who got swapped in a cradle and spent his life hewing and carrying while some other berk lived it up in wonderland—'Full of antimacassars,' he told himself, having heard the word in a production of some Victorian fol-de-rol at his school and held it ever after to his heart as the symbol of a world bright and shiny. If his father was of such grand lineage but would do nothing except belch Holden's Golden fumes at it, it was up to him to take up the cause in order

199

to…what? He didn't know or care. Aim and purpose were what teachers went on about and they belonged among the wooden people, coarse-grained, ignoble.

At some point he'd conceived the notion that Grace O'Malley sometimes tired of queenliness and was a pirate on the side. He spent more and more time at the local library, earning his mother's disapprobation at another dreamer in the tribe, another pay-packet lost before it was earned. Nothing he read, as far as he could understand it, supported the idea of Grace as a Long Jean Silver. In fact he was right but perhaps something—how he read, his own humour—hid the truth behind this first fancy about his queen.

First fancies can never be wholly unmade. Soon his spread further, seeking out other ferocious worthies of the age and finally coming to rest on Hernán Cortés, nemesis of the Aztecs. As with the Queen of Connacht, he read stumblingly of Cortés' ranging and roving, his parleys and suppressions. Perhaps inevitably, something piratical grew like a summer shadow around the man. Pete imagined Grace and Cortés routing puny ships of the line and bearing away all they carried, down to the last nail. Chronology was as nothing to him. So what if Grace was only seventeen when Cortés died? She was a quick learner. He died with a cutlass in his hand. Somewhere along the way Pete read that he'd taken time out to stare at some peak or other and whoever it was that wrote about it called him Stout Cortez. Easier to say out loud, that.

Meanwhile the exigencies of life pressed hard. Leaving school unqualified, Pete got this and that job, always the shuffler, the gofer, the one dispatched by sardonic elders to fetch a special screwdriver ('Gotta be sky-blue, my mon') or British Standard Whitworth fandangos ('Yer'll know 'em. Big T cut into the top. T for twat, all right?'). So it was that he ended up at Timperley's but with the good luck of starting at the same time as Dave Frankiewicz, who soon befriended him and, disinclined to take any crap from anyone, mostly ensured that none came the lanky dreamer's way.

On that raw New Year's Eve afternoon as the pair of them set about the last demolitions, feet came scurrying between the pallets stacked high to one side of the yard and a face framed by stringy hair broke in on their haphazard rhythms.

Dave and Pete looked up and grinned, Pete especially. 'Here's the bloody waster,' said Dave, his usual greeting to Bump Wilson, the vacation student, who'd come by his nickname dramatically when on his second day he'd nearly taken a stockroom door off its hinges with a pallet-trolley.

'Hiding out?' asked Pete, and Bump nodded.

Dave cocked his head: 'That tiles display again?' Bump stretched out his arm to show tile-dust up to his shoulder. But there was no time now for Dave's usual banter about rubbish students and taxpayers' money and the bollocks that was progressive rock. A more measured tread came towards them from another direction.

'Bugger,' said Bump and vanished just as a face was looming round the wall at the opposite side of the yard. Bump clattered against a far pallet. Pete coughed to cover the sound.

'Well, well. Almost forgot about you pair.' A figure stood before them with shaved head and hands thrust deep into a black puffer-jacket with *John Player Special* high across the chest. 'You haven't seen that streak of student piss, have you?'

'Out on a delivery,' said Dave, hoping that Bump would have the sense to hole up in the dispatch bay for the rest of the afternoon. He and Pete straightened their backs. 'What you want?'

Aside from being a foreigner, Cheshire way, Steve Basford had worked on the delivery vans before suddenly and inexplicably turning white-collar. Power had come late to him and he wielded it like a slapstick.

'Mr Arthur said'—a loving roll of the boss's first name—'if you haven't got this done by four you can leave it till Wednesday. But'—now a wagged finger—'that doesn't mean you can slack. Mr Arthur said,' he added quickly, for Dave was looking at him as though he were the last cistern in the yard. He backed away till he was safe. Then, 'Here, Hughes,' he called, 'what's this rubbish you're doing at the Arden tonight?'

Dave turned on Pete: 'How'd he find out? Were you practising in the basement like I said and said not to?'

'I couldn't help it. Wanted Bump to hear it through and he'd nearly finished his break. No time to find anywhere that—'

'Well you'd better not eat into our presentation'—*presentation* got the *Mr Arthur* treatment—"cos ours is ace.'

'Our presentation' was a scene from *The Shadows Cry for Death,* a whodunit from the Billy Bunn Players, whom Basford had recently joined and through whose ranks, work-style, he had swiftly risen. The fare they offered rarely strayed from a drawing-room and made frequent reference to things like antimacassars—though not in the dream-quickening way that Pete heard and whispered the word.

'Pete's'll be better than your bollocks,' called Dave but then, turning to Pete, 'do you really have to call yourself Ronan O'Malley for it?'

'Means little seal, you know, Ronan.' And Dave realised that, as always with Pete, he'd had it explained but not.

A huge upstairs room. Lots of velvet swagging and leftover Christmas decorations. A banner above the stage area, *Chas. Timperley, Builders' Merchants to the Trade, Est. 1920.* Chunky water-jugs on every table. Turkey-and-two-veg mostly, though some of the younger staff had gone for vindaloo or chow mein. Pints of Banks's or Harp, bulbous glasses of g&t, rum-and-black. Arthur and all the Timperleys at the top table, delicately forking things which might have been French. Variegated puds and then Mr Arthur's speech. Heartfelt thanks, the joke about his first day in the swivel-chair which never failed to exact its due. 'We worked like the bee in '73. Let's buzz some more in '74.' Applause, cheers, one elderly voice muttering sod that, they were still stalling about his pension.

The turns. 'The Ballad of Timperley Yard' by Mr Arthur's youngest, who had yet to set foot in it. Two secretaries and the wages clerk with a wayward medley of Slade and Gilbert O'Sullivan. The Billy Bunn crew were scheduled to finish up before the dancing. But now there was Pete.

There was Ronan. Breeches, wide-awake hat, jacket flared and velvet, red sash, cutlass in hand. He was transformed, magnificent, much to the relief of Bump Wilson, who'd put his offering through final revisions and, until it began, had been coiled like a spring beside an exasperated Dave and his wife. To dead silence, the ballad of Grace and Cortez unfolded and Pete's years of obsession made of his voice a thing apart. Grace and Cortez met amid the wafting winds of Hispaniola, she seventeen, he sixty-two. They avasted and belayed around the globe before ascending a peak in Darien ('Keats, that,' Bump had explained and Pete had said, wow, nice one). There, the greatest treasures of the world were hidden beneath the unwatchful eyes of dozing gods:

Plunging as one, their two hands did a-meet
To scoop and plunder, brave, defiant, fleet
Then to return…

But there was no return. A commotion erupted behind the swagging and an unknown voice said, 'Do it, he's gone on long enough' before Basford leapt at Pete in ill-fitting black tie: 'Aha, so there you are, my fine fellow! The parson said he'd seen some ne'er-do-well lurking at the lych-gate!'

'My, my,' said Mr Arthur, 'this is awfully good.' His table applauded palm-on-palm. Pete gawped and dropped his cutlass. His sash fell away. Dave was on his feet: 'Basford, you mad-arse!'

But Basford ploughed on uninventively—'Aha! Aha, I say!'—and the dagger was at Pete's chest. It was a theatrical dagger. The press of a catch slid the blade back into the handle. But Basford's power fogged his mind and eyes and sweated out over his hand.

Walking back from the jetty, Dave Frankiewicz recalls the apologetic look in the eyes of Pete's youngest brother when he stood on the doorstep. Pete's mother had wanted nothing to do with the ashes—'Like feyther like son—Waster!'—and they'd gone from hand to hand around the family before coming to rest with his youngest brother, who'd kept them forgotten in a shed. But now, 'See, it's impractical,' he'd said to Dave. 'I mean, you can't hang onto an urn and emigrate at the same time—can you?'

'Wished I'd had 'em first off,' said Dave, slamming the door shut as he spoke.

He'd kept them a long, loving time. But at last, with that anniversary coming up, forty years since the first about-time-too holiday, he judged it only right that his unfathomable pal should be returned to the town of his fathers in the land of the only woman who'd ever made his eyes mist up.

By the Garinish Island ticket office a figure comes towards him, tall and trim, no longer stringy-haired:

'All right, Dave?'

'All right, our Bump.'

'I phoned my sister. Her friends in Listowel say no problem for tonight so we'll be nice and early for Shannon.'

'Hope the Duty-Free's nice and early an' all. Expecting us any time, the friends?'

'Well…guess we should see the New Year in with them at least but…no, not specifically.'

'Sound.' Dave points across the street to The Beara Bar. 'Let's go up that Cortez peak, my mon, and get bladdered.'

The Maker's Mark

Mr Bryce favoured a slow body-swing with one leg hitched and, at the last minute, a scrunch of the shoulder. Miss Jerrold perched sideways first and then, knees tightly together, pivoted in, always brushing imaginary dust from her shoulder before she settled. Dean Grace went at it like a kid launching onto a bouncy castle. He had some last-minute moves, too: hand clamped to the frame, elaborate swerve of the bum. Often he'd finish with a quick tattoo on his knees. Nurse Lavender, long retired, was a clatter of sticks on metal, a slow worming-in, often a flap of the hand as if giving a ghost to understand that she'd managed before and would manage again, thank you kindly.

Whenever he could, Ian Wilkerson would watch from the landing window when any of the neighbours got into their cars. Their manoeuvres fascinated him. It offered such a narrow range of possibilities, the business of translating yourself from both feet on the ground to readiness for driving. But these neighbours had their signature ways. Sometimes they would even introduce a variant note, an extra wrestle with the belt, the decision to open and slam the door again when already it was properly closed. Ian knew their ways and was prepared for any variants. And in the unlikely event that he forgot, or later reflected that some variant was downright bizarre, his notebook would confirm that all was as he had witnessed.

By the time he was fourteen Ian had decided that the world was an unreliable place, apt to poke or blob out here and there like the duvets which, once their season was done, his mother tried to stuff away in their zipper-bags. So it was best kept at arm's length. You never knew when a friend, parted with on good terms the day before, might kick off inexplicably when next you met them. You never knew when some bus-driver, jolly as you like on a previous journey, might eff and jeff because you weren't holding your pass just right for their inspection. Or when some shopkeeper might sigh deeply because you hadn't got the exact change for your homeward treat.

As for his parents and teachers, they frequently defied second guessing. He often carried himself into class or through his front door in the manner of a lion-tamer, chair and whip at the ready, in case the lion wasn't dozing but braced to spring from the shadows. At fourteen he was beginning to fumble his way into some sense of cause and effect. The friend, the bus-driver, the parent, the teacher—any or all of them might be irritated by something that had nothing to do with him. He just happened by accident to be the target for their latest dart. That this was so, however, did not excuse it. Let them loose their darts on someone else or, best of all, into plain air.

So it was that he developed a liking for neutral actions—or at least, actions in which he played no part. Hence his love of monitoring the neighbours and how they got into their cars. And he found that keeping a log of all that offered a way of dealing with the other stuff, the unwarranted kerfuffle, the darts. By contrast, in another part of his notebook, he recorded the doings of those who came and kicked off and then went in his world. Anyone looking over his shoulder might have thought that here was an anthropologist in the making. It was nothing of the sort to Ian. It was to do with protection and control. Reducing someone's temper to a series of words on neatly ruled lines was a way of putting it in its place: a fact which gained immeasurably from shutting the book with a satisfying whump and storing it in a safe dark place.

Christmas was coming. On Saturday the 17th of December Ian had just put his bike in the garage when a familiar voice arrested his attention. He sped up to the landing, just in time to see Dean Grace defy all expectation as he waited for his wife and kids to get into the car for a shopping trip. Dean leaned against the open frame of the driver's door with his arms out, like a drunk, Ian later wrote, being patted down by night coppers. When everyone else was in the car Dean drew in his hands, pushed himself away from the frame, swivelled on his left foot and half-fell, half-folded into the driver's space as you might dump a boring present in a drawer. *Left foot-work has touch of Mr Bryce,* wrote Ian, *but faster as Dean G youngish and Mr B at least seventy.*

This choreography for a chill morning warmed Ian no end and certainly offset the parental mithering later in the day. *Dad's temper fair at lunch,* Ian wrote later, *but went all squally over the tree.* Ian's mother had her heart set on a change of tree that year and had seen just the thing in town the previous day. It was a shortish affair made of woody-looking plastic and covered with a sort of snow. It was certainly more manageable than the old tree, a whopper whose detachable branches were fixed to a

209

central trunk by colour-coded hooks. If you followed the code then voilà! you had the familiar pyramid of green. But the colour-tapes had mostly come off over time and last year the increasingly fractious attempts to create the pyramid had eaten up the best part of a day. *Dad banging on,* wrote Ian, *in way he calls bad manners when anyone else does it.*

For his father it was the old whopper or nothing. Too many cooks last year, he insisted. If he'd been alone with it there wouldn't have been any problem. He knew the length of the branches; those bits of coloured tape were just for the very first assembly. *Mum soon out-squalled him,* wrote Ian, and she certainly did, hissing that for an artificial tree it shed more needles than the real thing, that she was hoovering them up well into January. *Dad red as a beet,* wrote Ian. When his wrath found voice it was to insist that he'd show them, he'd have the old tree up in a trice—or he would if he could get at the garage shelf it was bundled up on. *Turned into my fault,* Ian wrote. *Bike always wedged in the way, plus he had devil's job getting at his toolbox and extension-leads. 'Wedged' is Dad-speak. I can move it no problem. But I said, ok, will move bike to other side of garage. Dad got redder, said it was really down to those fancy bike blocks I'd pestered them for and he wasn't giving himself a hernia moving them for me. I said, ok, will slide blocks out of the way and leave bike in hall, put newspaper under wheels. Then Mum red as a beet, says no use asking me to remember newspaper and how would it look to anyone at front door being greeted by dirty bike? Plus handlebars would mark wall.*

But the day ended on a happier note. Ian was dispatched to draw the upstairs curtains as it was starting to get dark. From the landing window he saw Miss Jerrold pull up, having brought her widowed sister from the station for what was now their Christmas routine. The passenger side was facing Ian and he was charmed by the fact that the sister's exit from the car was the mirror-image of Miss Jerrold's entry: brush of shoulder, knees tight, pivot out, and then a duck-and-stand whose grace made Ian think of a woodland nymph emerging from under a low broad leaf.

School didn't break up till Tuesday. On Monday morning the bus driver tugged Ian's hand across his little counter and appraised his pass so closely that Ian half-expected him to snatch it up and bite it. Then a couple of teachers had a quiet word about his progress, the kind that spreads a dull ache through an upcoming holiday. After the big assembly on Tuesday his friend Ade Rowley said that he couldn't go into town with him on Friday after all.

'What about between Christmas and New Year?' asked Ian.

'What about it?' shrugged Ade and then a ruck of genial boys bore him away.

At home the battle of the trees was lost and won. The old one was up—in a trice, said Ian's father, though no one had been around to see him wrestle it out of the garage and achieve the green pyramid—but Ian's mother had bought the other one for the front-room alcove. Neither was yet decorated but that was all right. *Cheski told them not to worry,* wrote Ian on Tuesday night. *She and that Alan will do both and she'll get extra bling for the small one. They'll be here tomorrow. Mum and Dad all smiles at Tuesday supper. Didn't even ask to see my term report right away. Dad called me 'young 'un'. Can't imagine Mr Bryce or Miss Jerrold using such language.*

Cheski, or Francesca, was twelve years older than Ian, had nearly died when she was a week old and, about a year later, nearly died again. She worked in a museum and was rising through the ranks. Alan had been her bloke for a while and Ian's mother and father liked him a lot. 'A keeper,' Ian's mother called him, and Cheski had hinted that he could be the one. Ian disliked him intensely. He was given to sideways comments and whispers when no one else was around. Ian couldn't get a complete handle on it but he sensed that, as a boy, Alan had been pretty useless and was now looking to balance things out by projecting that uselessness onto him. That, at least, seemed the simplest way to take him.

On Wednesday morning Mr Bryce rang some serious changes, stretching his arms and working his shoulders by the open door of his car and then getting in in a manner that somehow combined Miss Jerrold's elegance and Dean Grace's brio. *Like he was doing PE,* Ian later wrote. *Like he suddenly knows he's old.* Cheski and Alan arrived at lunchtime and by two o'clock the trees were fully bedizened. Cheski gave them chapter and verse on her progress at work. Alan asked to see Ian's school report.

'Oh, that,' said his father. 'Just been perusing it myself.'

'Perusing, is it?' said Alan. 'That good, eh?' There was laughter all round, almost, and something in Cheski's laugh seemed to confirm Ian's fears that Alan might indeed be the one. His father ended on a chuckle: 'Oh yes, that good. Now where did I put the thing?'

Ian said he'd look for it, swept it up from the hall table where it had been lying since morning, went up to his room and hid it in a bottom drawer. His father had been tippling since before Cheski and Alan arrived. With any luck, the report's disappearance would be laughingly attributed to his low-grade befuddlement. Coming back, he heard an engine and, from the landing window, saw the Graces' car pulling up. Its door slowly opened and Mrs Grace languidly emerged. Ian watched as she closed the door and, hand on hip, bent down to rub at something by the handle. He couldn't find words for how he felt, except to recall how his Art teacher had waxed lyrical about some painting called *The Birth of Venus*. But then a harsh *Pssst!* crushed his reverie and he saw Alan at the foot of the stairs.

'What you doing?'

'I thought I saw a buzzard.'

'Oh, yeah? Buzzard? Cheski said you're a Nosey Norman.' It baffled Ian that his sister seemed to reach back to a time before their parents were born for her terms of non-endearment to him. Maybe museum-work did that to you. 'Anyway,' continued Alan, 'got that report of yours?'

Ian shook his head. 'Dad was in the garage earlier. I'll have a look there.' He flew down the stairs, caught Alan's hiss of, 'Bet you were checking out some fit babe,' and got himself out of the house.

He contrived to keep himself out over most of the next two days. Friends to see, he said, plus he needed to read up on some things at the library. Given those balefully quiet words from his teachers, the latter was at least a nod to the truth. The library was in the centre of town and recently refurbished. You took an escalator up to the floor for Special Collections, Reference, Local Interest. More important for Ian, the second floor had big wide windows with an unimpeded view of the on-street parking and, dead opposite, the Pay-and-Display car park. Ian settled himself into a comfy chair right by the window and got out his notebook.

Almost immediately he was rewarded. A car came out of the Pay-and-Display and stopped. Along the street came a woman, lolloping in that way people have when you keep a door open for them while they're still yards away. The driver leaned over and opened the passenger door. When the woman reached it she bent sideways like someone being a tree in a school play and flew in as if by suction. Moments later a young man returned to his car at the side of the street. He stood hands on hips before the bonnet, then buffed the insignia in a way that disarmingly reminded Ian of Mrs Grace. That done, he strode round to the driver's side and sort of wove his way in like a genie vanishing through the neck of a bottle. Ian could see his face through the windscreen. It was all smiles. OK, maybe he'd just had some good news but Ian liked to think that, really, he was gratified at his nifty moves. As the hours passed, motorists of all stripes kept him similarly absorbed with manoeuvres all the way from willowy to robotic.

At last a librarian came up and announced fifteen minutes to closing. Gathering his coat and bag—and

214

having a quick look at an atlas so he could say that schoolwork hadn't gone completely by the board—Ian pondered all the shows that were daily put on for him. It wasn't just a matter of people being older than him and thus licensed to drive. It was about the power to decide which landscape to inhabit and when. Getting into a car was a way of saying, I was in the mess of the world and now I'm in my refuge, where noise is muffled and all around is just so many cartoons. Getting out was a way of saying I'm strong enough to take on the mess for a bit. And the way each person dropped something unique into that literally narrow range of moves—it was like a painter's initials or one of those whatever-they-were on a jewellery setting or something antique. A thingy mark. Maker's, that was it.

And of course there was the wonderful freedom. I'll go from A to B via J; no I won't, I'll go via Z; no, forget A and B, what would D to G feel like? No one yapping any more about me wedging my bike where they can't get at stuff. Or maybe, forget A and Z and all in between…I'll just go.

'That you, Ian?' called his mother as he came in the front door.

'Been studying hard?' called Cheski from the front room.

'Been in the dirty books section?' whispered Alan on one of his gratuitous scurries through the hall. He'd always go straight from A to B, Ian decided. He wouldn't know anything else. And he'd grind the gears.

Ian went upstairs and sat on his bed. He thought of that young man again, all smiles at securing his safety. He

215

started to feel pleased with himself in just the same way. He always watched his mother and father closely as they checked the handbrake and ensured the car was in neutral, turned the ignition and depressed the clutch, as they found first or reverse as the situation required, went up and down the gears as conditions and limits dictated. He went through it all himself, remembering with a happy thrill that the new car had a little green prompt to the right of the speedometer: *Shift,* it said, if you were running too hard in a lower gear or dropping speed in a higher. A quiet little light with its unfussy word. Shift. Which of course could mean much more than manipulating speed.

On Friday night Cheski and Alan took them out for a meal. The place was on the posh side so Ian's choice, pizza, allowed everyone to indulge despair in a kind of part-song:

'Oh, he does let me down': mother's fake trill.

'At Christmastime?': Dad's eye moist above his wine-glass.

'Don't you wolf enough of those?': Cheski suddenly twice her years.

'Don't they teach you about proper food?': Alan the community leader, then, lower, with elbow-nudge, 'Or are you in the cloakroom watching porn?'

But the waiter, hovering, said that Ian's choice was a speciality and they all stared at Ian once he'd gone as though he'd bribed the man to say it. But more mileage awaited with Ian's side order.

'Oh, no,' he insisted to Alan's am-dram frown, 'I like salad.'

'So a rubbishy main and a healthy side.' Alan snorted and had a swig of his water. 'The guy's on drugs.' Ian assumed that he intended an American accent but he sounded like a parrot on helium.

'Always been a Dozy Derek'—Cheski gave him a dead stare—'haven't you?'

'Well, keep it on the side dish,' said his father. 'We know what you're like in public places.'

'Ooh, sounds bad. Streaking, was he?' Now Alan went for a mock-tremor, at which Cheski nudged him from the other side and called him a right one.

'Oh, now, now,' said Ian's mother, the usual extent of her defence of their second, belated child. 'But mind you ask the chappie for one of those special sharp knives, Ian,' she added, making Ian picture the waiter as he revolved above them in slow-motion before splitting the table with a gem-encrusted sword.

As it turned out, he forgot to ask and, never keen on working between two plates, transferred half of the salad onto his pizza. Not that it mattered. The others clattered on, heads bowed, and roved between sundry topics, none of which were turned his way. His father called for more wine. Picturing the descent of the sword again, Ian forked the rest of the salad into the space left by his disappearing pizza. Then Alan started on about some big news.

'Do tell,' said Ian's mother, staring at but apparently not seeing the errant salad on his pizza-plate.

'Well.' Cheski dabbed at her lips with her napkin. 'It's not a hundred percent definite but I think…think, mind you'—and she stared round the table with a cat-plus-

217

cream look—'that the job I mentioned is in the bag.'

'Oh, darling, you'll be just down the road,' bellowed Ian's father and waved like a delirious tic-tac man for yet more wine even though the last bottle was still half-full.

'We're starting to…you know'—uncharacteristically, Alan went all aw-shucks—'look around. Something suitable.'

Ian's mother clapped her hands. His father emptied the current bottle all round and hoicked the new one out of the waiter's hands. Ian's knife and fork stopped. Starting to look around. Something suitable. He understood. Both of them never not in the house and months and years of Alan's pervy undertones. Anger found his hands and he dug deep into the pizza. The salad sprayed over the table-cloth. Disgust and admonition came thick and fast but Ian caught not one word. And anyway, all the words fell back before one single image: Alan leaning close in, too close, lifting Ian's knife and fork from his fingers and slowly, deliberately, like parent with toddler, cutting the remainder of the pizza into bite-size triangles: 'There,' he said when he'd finished. 'And if you ask nicely the man might clear up your mess and bring you some fresh salad…to stay on its own plate.'

Ian looked to his mother and father for something…anything: rogue indulgence, unwitting affection, even just the bland remark that everyone was young once. But his mother and Cheski were shaking their heads at each other as though playing mirrors and his father's head was in his hands, though that didn't stop a hand from stretching to top up his glass. Alan placed

218

Ian's knife and fork back on the plate side by side and patted his shoulder. The pat lingered.

That night Ian lay in bed and watched everything fall together. OK, Christmas would be do-able because he sort of wouldn't be there. There'd be the super-bright jollity, father's early tippling, no, let's not fart about, father's alcoholism, and mother and Cheski in the kitchen and Alan nipping in to help and probably joke about being ready to cut up a certain person's plateful all neat and tidy, but he could weather that, and all the ooh-and-aah of the presents, and the Queen saying much the same as this time last year, and the meal and probably jokes about flying sprouts and gravy, but he could weather that too, and then Alan and his father's joint hogging of the remote and his father passing out around seven if not before. But he could stay off to the side…literally…say, beside the old whopper of a tree…so that Alan would find it mighty difficult to home in with more rubbish on his lips. Really, it would be like watching people get into and out of their cars. And he imagined himself looking down on the living room for the whole day from an invisible landing window.

But a do-able Christmas still wasn't much cop. And then there was after. A whole new year to be got through. And it wouldn't be long before his birthday, so there'd be all that fifteen-ness to get through as well. And at some point, sooner rather than later, Cheski would phone or turn up with confirmation of her good news and shortly after that the pair of them would be staying again, for a weekend, and another and another, and Alan and his father would get all deep-voiced about whatever it was that you had to consider, whether a house had damp, how close it was to whatever it had to be close to, and you wouldn't be able to move for words like 'agent' and 'solicitor' and the living room floor would be covered with pictures of flats and semis and bungalows and detacheds and there'd be big chat about—Ian dredged up bits and ends from a Civic Awareness lesson, 'How We All Live'—yes, about desirable locations and what made something much sought after. And each time Alan would know when Ian was moving from A to B, or G to R, when he was alone in open country, and all the while Ian's mother and father would look while not looking, hear while not hearing, blind as bats and deaf as posts because Alan was a keeper. And he cut food up ever so nice.

The memory of his father's voice echoed out of the dark: 'No, it'll be safe enough outside. Never any trouble round here.' Alan had driven the car home, having stayed fastidiously under the limit. 'Besides, you'd only have to do battle with his pest of a bike. Just pop the fob thing on that bowl there.'

'Alan bought us that,' echoed his mother. 'Last time he came.'

'Really?'

'Oh, I did tell you.'

'Well, that's damned thoughtful of you, sir.'

After a long moment Ian got up, went to his window and double-checked. A little later, dressed, rucksack full, money-box empty, he was out of the silent house and standing at the kerb. This was it. Time to fashion his own maker's mark. OK, over the years it would change but, as some of his school-friends were apt emptily to boast, you never forget your first time. He'd have to move quick: the *chhk-chhk* of the lock might bring a light on. Where would he go? He hadn't thought. No, come on…hadn't he? Christmas, this town like any other, refuges, hostels. There'd been collections galore for them in the last two weeks at school, their literature piled and pinned up along the main entrance. Half a dozen of them at least. He'd recognise the names, the places. But it wouldn't be clever to chauffeur himself right to any door. He wouldn't want any complications getting in the way with the kind face, the listening ear. So, Ian, what's this chap's name? And why is he at your house? And can you…can you tell me the kind of things he says, Ian? Though he might call himself something different, just to start with. Ade, maybe. If that Rowley had withdrawn his friendship, the least he could leave was his name.

Right then. Find one of them, park a way off, drop the fob down a drain and walk back. As he was thinking this a light did come on, upstairs at the Graces'. *Chhk-chhk* and he was in. The seat only needed one click forward. Footwell, gearstick, the reach to pedals and wheel—all the space and shapes felt like they'd been waiting for right now. And the way he'd swung in, touching neither door nor frame—what was that but a move in its true moment?

By the time Dean Grace opened the front door Ian was taking his first roundabout like an old, old hand.

About the Author

Novels

The Mercury Annual (TQF / Theaker's Paperback Library, 2009)

Pilgrims at the White Horizon (TQF / Theaker's Paperback Library, 2013)

Short fiction

The Portswick Imp: Collected Stories, 2001-2016 (Black Pear Press, 2018)

Sing Ho! Stout Cortez: Novellas and Stories (Black Pear Press, 2021)

Poetry collections

God's Machynlleth and Other Poems (Flarestack, 1996)

Port Winston Mulberry (Littlejohn and Bray, 2009)

Batman's Hill, South Staffs (Flipped Eye International, 2013)

The Girl from Midfoxfields (Black Pear Press, 2014)

Come To Pass (Oversteps Books, 2014)

Early and Late (Cairn Time Press, 2018)

Featured in Polly Stretton, ed, *The Unremembered: World War One's Army of Workers, The British Story* (Black Pear Press, 2018)

The Stations of the Day (Black Pear Press, 2019)

Under Smoky Light (Offa's Press, 2020)

Journals: publication in such journals as *The Antioch Review* (US), *The Antigonish Review* (Canada), *Critical Survey, Crossroads* (Poland), *The English Review, The London Magazine, Magazine Six* (US), *Muscadine Lines* (US), *Other*

Poetry, Pennine Platform, Poetry Salzburg Review, The Scarlet Leaf Review (Canada), *Stand, Under the Radar.*

Drama
Assumption Eve (Worcester Commandery, 2000)
FAQ (The Progress Theatre Festival, Reading, 2009, and the Shoebox Theatre Company, Staffordshire, 2011)
When? (The Blue Orange Theatre, Birmingham [Shoebox Theatre Company], 2011)

Novellas
Esp. Shortlisted for the UK Novella Award (2015)
Tickle, Tickle. Toronto: *The Scarlet Leaf Review* (Autumn 2019)

Essays and Reviews
1996-present: *Critical Survey, Crossroads, English, The English Review, The Explicator, Irish Studies Review, The Irish University Review, The Journal of American Haiku, The London Magazine, No Limits, Other Poetry, Staple Magazine, The Times Literary Supplement, Under the Radar.*

www.michaelwthomas.co.uk
The Swan Village Reporter:
http://swansreport.blogspot.co.uk/

Acknowledgements

The author and publisher gratefully acknowledge the following:

- *Esp* was shortlisted for The UK Novella Award, 2015.
- *Tickle Tickle* appeared in *The Scarlet Leaf Review* (Toronto: September 2019).
- 'Never Any Sometimes' appeared in *Whispering Dialogue* (April 2019).
- 'Sing Ho! Stout Cortez' appeared in *Dark Lane Anthology 8* (2019).

Special thanks to Black Pear Press and Katherine Dixson at Way Beyond Words for expert advice and proofing, and to Ted Eames for the cover illustration.